GUYS READ

FUNNY
BUSINESS

GUYS READ

FUNNY BUSINESS

EDITED AND WITH AN INTRODUCTION BY
JON SCIESZKA

STORIES BY
**MAC BARNETT, EOIN COLFER,
CHRISTOPHER PAUL CURTIS, KATE DiCAMILLO &
JON SCIESZKA, PAUL FEIG, JACK GANTOS,
JEFF KINNEY, DAVID LUBAR, ADAM REX,
AND DAVID YOO**

WITH ILLUSTRATIONS BY
ADAM REX

WALDEN POND PRESS
An Imprint of HarperCollinsPublishers

Walden Pond Press® is an imprint of HarperCollins Publishers.

Walden Pond Press and the skipping stone logo are trademarks and registered trademarks of Walden Media, LLC.

Library of Congress Cataloging-in-Publication Data
Guys read : funny business / edited and with an introduction by Jon Scieszka ; stories by Mac Barnett . . . [et al.] ; with illustrations by Adam Rex. — 1st ed.
    v. cm.
Summary: A collection of humorous stories featuring a teenaged mummy, a homicidal turkey, and the world's largest pool of chocolate milk.
    Contents: Best of friends / Mac Barnett — Will / Adam Rex — Artemis begins / Eoin Colfer — Your Question for Author Here / Kate DiCamillo & Jon Scieszka — A fistful of feathers / David Yoo — Unaccompanied minors / Jeff Kinney — Kid appeal / David Lubar — What? You think you got it rough? / Christopher Paul Curtis — My parents give my bedroom to a biker / Paul Feig — The bloody souvenir / Jack Gantos.
    ISBN 978-0-06-196374-2 (trade bdg.) — ISBN 978-0-06-196373-5 (pbk. bdg.)
    1. Children's stories, American. 2. Humorous stories, American. [1. Humorous stories. 2. Short stories.] I. Scieszka, Jon. II. Rex, Adam, ill. III. Title: Funny business.
PZ5.G96 2010   2010008122
[Fic]—dc22   CIP
                                                                      AC

Typography by Joel Tippie
10 11 12 13 14   LP/RRDB   10 9 8 7 6 5 4 3 2 1
❖
First Edition

CONTENTS

BEFORE WE BEGIN . . .

A kid gets transferred to a new school. He's at lunch the first day. A sixth grader yells out, "Thirty-seven!" Everybody starts laughing. A seventh grader yells, "Fifty-one!" Even bigger laughs. The new kid asks his classmate sitting next to him at the lunch table, "What the heck is going on?" The guy says, "Well, we've got only one joke book in the library. And everybody has read it a million times. So now instead of telling the whole joke, all we have to do is yell out the number of the joke. Everybody gets it. It saves a lot of time."

The new kid thinks this is a pretty funny idea. He goes down to the library, checks out the joke book, and memorizes three of the funniest jokes and their numbers.

The next day at lunch, the same thing happens. A fifth grader yells out, "Forty-four!" Lots of laughs. An eighth grader yells, "Twenty-seven!" Huge laughs. The new kid calls out his favorite, "Thirty-eight!" Nothing. Dead silence. Nobody laughs. The new kid turns to his classmate and says, "What happened?" The guy shrugs and answers, "Some people just can't tell a joke."

And some people just can't write humor. Those people are not in this book. Because Guys Read believes that humor is seriously one of the best kinds of reading. Humor is important. To get why something is funny, you have to first understand the thing itself, then understand why changing it in an unexpected way is funny. Your brain is doing some great work when it's laughing.

It was E. B. White, a pretty funny guy, who once said, "Humor can be dissected, as a frog can, but the thing dies in the process, and the innards are discouraging to any but the pure scientific mind." So we won't do any more dissection. We'll just let you know you are in for a raging robot, a homicidal turkey, a bloody souvenir, a biker taking over a kid's bedroom, and more, by some of the best and funniest writers around.

And one more bit of good news before you dive into the funny business: this is just Volume 1 of the multivolume

Guys Read Library. Each volume will cover one genre, with a bunch of the best writers and illustrators contributing original pieces of Nonfiction, Action/Adventure, Sci-Fi/Fantasy, Thriller/Mystery, Sports, and Who Knows.

But we do know that every Guys Read Library book will be packed with the kind of writing guys will enjoy, the kind of writing that gives guys a reason to want to be readers.

Check out www.guysread.com for more news . . . and more recommendations of good stuff.

And always remember: "Eighty-seven!"

Jon Scieszka

GUYS READ

FUNNY
BUSINESS

BEST OF FRIENDS
BY MAC BARNETT

Ernest was a nerd, but it was fourth grade: we were all nerds. Even the best of us were shackled to some fatal flaw. James, who was the fastest kid in the class, was also the last one to carry a lunch box. Jean-Pierre had already started cutting the sleeves off his gym shirts, but he hadn't yet started going by J.P.: even little Tim Houston wasn't afraid to put on a French accent and say "Jean-Pierre, *oui oui*" when they stood next to each other in line. And me? I was terrible at sports, last picked for everything. At recess I hung out on the sidelines of the basketball court and bet kids quarters that they couldn't make free throws. (I usually cleared a few bucks a week.) It was there, on the sidelines, that I would sometimes talk to Ernest.

Ernest looked more ninety than nine. He had thick-lensed glasses that were attached snugly to his face by a cloth band that wrapped around his head. Our school had uniforms, and he was the only kid to opt for the cardigan instead of the sweater. Twin deposits of dried spit lined either side of his mouth; he always looked like he had just eaten lots of vanilla frosting.

Sometimes you'd feel bad for Ernest, but he'd always do something to mess it up. Example: in kindergarten I'd let him sit next to me in art. One day I was drawing a picture of a veterinarian, and in the middle of our conversation, Ernest leaned over and drew a long oval in between the guy's legs. I was dumbstruck.

And so I missed Ms. Maxwell coming up behind us.

"Lovely picture, Ernest," she said. He'd drawn Freddy Krueger battling Jason battling a Ninja Turtle underneath a fleet of stealth bombers. All the guys in his drawing had too many muscles—it looked like they had three biceps on each arm.

And then: "Dean, what's that?"

Ms. Maxwell's tone was strange, like her throat was tight.

I tilted my head straight back so I was looking right up at Ms. Maxwell's chin. She was looking down at my paper.

"It's a veterinarian?" I said. "You know, a vet? Someone

who takes care of animals?"

"I know what a veterinarian is, Dean," said Ms. Maxwell. "What's that?" She frowned and pointed to Ernest's contribution to the piece.

"Oh," I said. "He dropped a hot dog."

"A hot dog?"

"Yeah, he was eating a hot dog and he dropped it. So now it's falling to the ground." I started to draw a hot dog bun in the hand that wasn't holding a stethoscope.

"Oh," said Ms. Maxwell. "That's very silly." She believed me, but I think only because she didn't want to believe the alternative.

Ms. Maxwell moved on to another table. Ernest collapsed onto folded arms, giggling. As he shook with laughter, the end of the cloth band wriggled like a tadpole's tail on the back of his head.

Ernest.

Things hadn't changed much since then. That was the thing with Ernest: as soon as you tried to be nice to him, he made you regret it.

But before I keep going about what Ernest did, I have to tell you a little bit about the first-best television commercial that year. In case you're wondering, the third-best television commercial was for some sort of G.I. Joe watercraft. The kids in the commercial had an elaborate system of aqueducts in their room that basically looked like a real miniature swamp, and the ad made it seem like the toy was self-propelled. Joe's boat slammed into and capsized Cobra Commander's hovercraft and then jacked up onto a sandy beach, at which point two kids popped up from behind a line of miniature mangrove trees and shouted, "Go, Joe!" I didn't even like G.I. Joes, but I wanted a swamp in my room.

The second-best commercial of the year was for a board game called Crossfire. It started with two kids—one with an edgy, spiky haircut—entering a futuristic gladiator arena. At the center of the arena was the Crossfire game board, which looked like a tiny plastic version of the same arena the boys were standing in. The kids started playing Crossfire, which involved shooting silver ball bearings at a ninja star in the middle of the arena. There were five intense seconds of stuff flying around and colliding while some invisible guy just shredded on an electric guitar and screamed "Crossfire!" over and over. Finally the spiky-haired kid threw his hands in the air and said, "I win!" This commercial was notable not just for being heart-spasmingly intense but also because it was pretty much the only board-game commercial I ever saw where the winning kid didn't have a dorky bowl cut.

But the number-one best commercial of the year was so much better than these two runner-ups. The competition wasn't even close. It was an ad for Nesquik Chocolate Syrup, and it was the kind of thing that would make you drop your Pop-Tart and run in from the kitchen if you heard it come on in the other room. The ad took place in the Nesquik factory. It started with an establishing shot of the building that looked like it was taken from a helicopter or maybe from a powerful camera attached to a satellite orbiting Earth. A voice invites you to see what's going on inside. The camera zooms in fast until it passes through the walls, and then we see a rapid-fire procession of scenes from the factory's belly. Conveyer belts sending an endless parade of chocolate candy to be melted into chocolate syrup, shiny metal instruments spewing liquid chocolate like geysers—that kind of thing. It was amazing, exactly what you hoped a chocolate milk factory would be like. But the best part, the part that got stuck in your mind until it was melted and processed into the stuff of chocolate daydreams, was the ending. A kid in swim trunks leaps into what seems to be the mouth of an ordinary waterslide but turns out to be a huge, twisty-straw-shaped waterslide. He plummets around and around the straw's dizzying red-and-white-striped spirals until he lands, delighted, in a giant pool of cool, delicious chocolate milk. Other kids are in the pool with him, laughing and splashing around. A guy from the Nestlé corporation with long blond hair and a whistle is there to act as a lifeguard, but you can tell by the way he's smiling that he'll pretty much let you get away with anything.

It was fantastic.

I wanted to ride down that waterslide into that pool of chocolate milk so badly. Everyone did. We talked about it at lunch. We thought about it in class. Sometimes the kids who didn't play sports would act it out during recess. I wished—and I wasn't the only one—that somehow one day I could gain access to that factory.

I thought maybe if I made enough money, I could bribe my way into the chocolate milk pool. And so my betting at the basketball courts took on a new urgency. One Friday morning at recess, I was standing courtside while James shot. He had just made a free throw, and I was twenty-five cents in the hole.

"Double or nothing," I said.

"Okay," said James.

Usually the prospect of doubling your money was enough to break your concentration. The ball bounced off the rim. We were even.

"Again," he said.

"Sure."

James shot and missed.

"Double or nothing," said James.

"Okay."

He missed.

I saw Ernest trudging up to the sidelines. I could tell he was excited about something because he kept opening and closing his mouth like an eel.

"Again?" James said.

"Hey, Dean," said Ernest.

"Hold on, Ernest," I said.

"Dean, I've got to tell you something. It's important."

James dribbled. He was getting too much time to focus.

"Dean," said Ernest.

James shot, and the ball made a lovely arc and went in the hoop.

"We're even!" said James.

"I didn't agree to that bet!" I shouted.

"We're even!" James ran around the court, pumping his fist.

"Dean," said Ernest.

I slowly turned to Ernest. "What?"

Ernest opened and closed his mouth a couple times

before he began. "You know that one commercial?"

I figured he was talking about Nesquik. We'd discussed the ad a couple times before. But I was annoyed.

"What commercial?" I said.

"The one for Nesquik? Where they go to the chocolate factory and stuff and the kids go down that straw and swim in chocolate milk and stuff?"

"Yeah, Ernest. I know that commercial. You know I know that commercial." James was shooting around with some kids from the older grades. Pretty soon they'd have a game going and then there'd be no chance to make some money. "What about it?"

Ernest gave an open-mouthed grin and the corners of his mouth glistened whitely in the sun. "I won the Nesquik sweepstakes."

I tensed. "What?"

"I won the Nesquik sweepstakes," he said again.

"What sweepstakes?" I didn't know there had been any sweepstakes. I suddenly felt angry at my mom. She never bought me Nesquik even though I always asked her for it. Instead we got Black and Gold Chocolate Milk Powder. The tin was yellow (not gold) with black lettering, and it looked like the kind of chocolate milk mix they must have used in the trenches of World War I.

"The Nesquik sweepstakes," Ernest said. For the third time.

"What's the prize?" I asked. My body was still. My heart had paused; my lungs had stopped filling. I thought I knew, but I wanted to hear it from Ernest's mouth.

"I get to go to the Nesquik factory and stuff."

Unbelievable.

"I get a plane trip and hotel and stuff and a ticket to the factory and I get to spend an hour in the waterslide part."

Fury washed over me. Ernest? Ernest won a ticket to the Nestlé factory? Ernest wasn't even allowed to watch much TV, so he had seen the commercial only once. One time. He'd told me this. And Ernest had never even been down a waterslide. He was afraid of heights *and* got motion sickness. How was he supposed to ride down the twisty straw? I wasn't even sure Ernest knew how to swim. He'd probably just doggy-paddle over to the edge of the pool, then get out and lie there sputtering like a turned-over turtle. And now he was sitting there grinning at me, the Nesquik sweepstakes winner.

"And guess what?" Ernest said, still smiling. "I get to bring a friend."

I smiled back.

"Seriously?" I asked.

"Seriously," said Ernest. "Cool, right?"

"That's really cool," I said, then paused to scratch my head. "Who are you going to bring?"

Ernest adjusted his glasses. "Well, it's hard. I have so many great friends and stuff—"

"Sure," I said. "Sure."

"So I'm just going to have to think and stuff and pick whoever in the class is my best friend, you know."

"Yes," I said. "I know."

"I figure I'll make my decision next Friday."

One week. I had one week.

"Ernest, who else have you told about the sweepstakes?"

Ernest looked surprised. "Just you."

"Good," I said. "That's good. You probably should keep it secret for now. Otherwise everybody might just kiss up to you and pretend to be your friend so they can get that ticket."

Ernest nodded slowly. "Yeah, you're right. That's good advice."

"Sure, Ernest."

"Thanks, Dean. You're a good friend."

"Yeah," I said. I clapped Ernest on the shoulder.

At lunch I traded Ernest my fruit snacks for actual fruit, a sucker's bargain if I'd ever made one. Then I invited him to sit with me and Brandon and Mark even though lunch conversation with Ernest was almost always a disaster.

"Want to hear a joke?" Ernest asked while Brandon was in the middle of a story. He didn't wait for us to answer. "When is a horse not a horse?"

We were silent.

"When he turns into a pasture!"

I looked at Brandon and Mark, who sat there staring at Ernest. Then I started laughing. Hard.

"Good one, Ernest!" I said. "Oh, man. That's a real good one. I'll have to use that one. I'll give you credit of course. . . . A pasture!"

Now Brandon and Mark were staring at me.

"Looks like these guys don't get it," I said, pointing my thumb at my two closest friends. "Not really up to our level, humor-wise, Ernest."

Ernest nodded energetically.

Brandon shook his head and pulled a Nesquik drink box out of his lunch bag.

I saw Ernest look at it. He opened his mouth to say something.

I stuffed my cookie into my backpack.

"Ernest, let's go play four square," I said.

"But there's only two of us," said Ernest.

"Then let's play two square."

"I've never heard of that."

"I'll show you," I said.

Ernest and I spent the rest of lunch bouncing a ball slowly back and forth.

"What kind of horse only comes out at night?" Ernest asked.

It was raining after school. We all stood under the overhang by the parking lot waiting for our parents to pick us up. Ernest's mom pulled up in a blue station wagon.

"Bye, buddy," I said as Ernest trudged out to his car.

"Bye, Dean," said Ernest.

We waved at each other.

"Later, Ernest," said James.

I snapped my head toward James. He gave Ernest a little two-fingered salute.

"Bye, James," said Ernest.

"See ya, Ernest," said Kim.

I turned around behind me. She was waving enthusiastically.

"Bye, dude," said Angelo.

"Bye, Ernest!" said Tiffany.

"Bye," said Adam.

"Bye," said Jean-Pierre.

"Bye, Ernest!" said Matt. "You're the man!"

Ernest turned around and smiled at everyone. He stood in the rain and waved. Droplets of water collected on his forehead and glasses, but he didn't seem to care. "Bye, everyone," he said.

His mom honked the horn. Ernest turned around and hustled over to her.

And even as the station wagon pulled out of the parking lot and disappeared down the road, everyone still waved.

This was not good.

As soon as I got home from school, I got out the class directory and dialed Ernest's number.

"Ernest!" I said. "You want to come over to my house for dinner tonight?"

"I'd love to and stuff, but I can't," he said. "I'm going to Fresh Mex."

"Fresh Mex?" I asked. "You mean Chevys?"

"Yeah," said Ernest.

The restaurant was called Chevys. Their slogan was Fresh Mex. Who called Chevys Fresh Mex?

Ernest.

"Who are you going to Chevys with?" I asked. "Your mom?"

"Yeah," said Ernest. "And Jean-Pierre."

My grip tightened around the receiver. Jean-Pierre? Jean-Pierre never even talked to Ernest. And now they were having Fresh Mex together?

"Ernest," I said. "Did you tell anyone else about the sweepstakes?"

Silence. Then: "Yes."

"Who did you tell?"

"Everybody."

"Ernest!" I said. "I told you not to— Never mind. That's fine." I changed up my tone. "Hey. I just realized. This is crazy: My mom and I are going to Chevys tonight, too!"

There was a pause, and then Ernest said, "I thought you were having dinner at home?"

"What?" I asked.

"You just invited me to your house for dinner."

"I invited you to come over to my house so we could drive over to Chevys for dinner."

"Oh," said Ernest. "Cool! Maybe we'll see you there!"

"I think you will," I said. "What time are you going?"

"Five thirty."

"Us, too," I said. "See you there, Ernest."

"Bye, Dean."

I hung up the phone.

"Mom!" I shouted up the stairs. "Can we please go to Chevys for dinner tonight?"

By the time I convinced my mom and we got to Chevys, Ernest and his mom and Jean-Pierre were already seated at a table. They were laughing and eating chips and they didn't see us come in.

"Two for dinner?" asked the hostess, whose name tag identified her as "Jennie O'Brien, Fiesta Animal."

"Four," I said, before my mom could answer.

She seated us at a large red booth in the corner. Immediately I got up and went over to Ernest's table.

"A *night* mare!" Ernest was saying as I approached.

Jean-Pierre laughed. "That's good, man. That's good." He held up his hand for a high five.

"Hey, guys!" I said.

"Hey, Dean!" said Ernest. Jean-Pierre just glared at me.

Ernest introduced me to his mom. "I've never talked to so many of Ernest's school friends as I have today!" she said, delighted.

"Great. That's great," I said. "Hey—I'm here with my mom. We should combine tables."

"The more the merrier, right?" said Ernest's mom.

"Right!" said Ernest.

"I kind of like this table," said Jean-Pierre quietly.

Ernest ignored him. "Dinner with two good friends!"

"We're at that booth over there," I said. "It doesn't really have room for five, but maybe we can pull up a chair for you, Jean-Pierre."

We headed toward our table, where my mom was sitting with a confused expression. I let Ernest and his mother get a few feet ahead and grabbed Jean-Pierre by the arm.

"I know what you're doing," I said.

Jean-Pierre quickly took my fingers off his arm. "Shut up, man. I know what *you're* doing."

"There's no way you're swimming in that chocolate pool."

"Wrong."

"You're not even Ernest's friend."

"Wrong again," said Jean-Pierre. "I'm Ernest's best friend. He just told me five minutes ago."

"Seriously?"

"Seriously."

"He used those words? 'Best friend'?"

Jean-Pierre smirked. "Yep. Well, he said 'best of friends.'"

I breathed out through my nostrils. Ernest.

Ernest turned around. "Come on, guys," he said. "What are you lollygagging around for, you sacks of potatoes?"

"Sacks of potatoes," I said, laughing. "That's a good one, Ernest."

Jean-Pierre mouthed something to me that I pretended not to understand.

Ernest and I were sitting next to each other in a booth while our moms talked. Jean-Pierre had left for the bathroom a few minutes earlier, which was fine with me.

"It's nice to spend time with another adult for once," Ernest's mom was saying.

"Yes," said my mom. "Sometimes I feel like my only company is grade-schoolers."

They laughed. I didn't. Ernest did, but he laughed whenever someone else laughed.

"You know," said Ernest's mom, "I had no idea those two were such good friends."

"Neither did—"

"Sure we are," I interrupted. "Ernest and I go way back. We were art buddies back in kindergarten, right?"

"Yeah," said Ernest. Then he started chuckling. "Hey, how much money does a bronco have?"

I tried to smile. "How much?"

Before he could answer, Jean-Pierre returned with a little paper bag in his right hand. He tossed it over to Ernest, who missed the catch. The brown sachet flopped onto his lap.

"Here you go, man," he said. "I got you some fresh tortillas from that machine over there."

Ernest pulled out a tortilla. "They're still warm and stuff! Thanks, Jean-Pierre!"

"Don't get too excited," I said. "It's not a big deal. Those are free, you know."

"So?" said Jean-Pierre. He gave me a threatening look.

I shrugged but didn't say anything. I had never been in a fight, and I sure wasn't going to start with Jean-Pierre.

Ernest, mouth full, looked at his mom. "Can I ask them?" he said.

"Of course," she said.

I held my breath. *Them?* Did Ernest have two tickets to the Nesquik factory?

"Do you guys want to come over for a sleepover?"

Jean-Pierre made a face like he was in pain. "Can't," he said. "I have a basketball tournament this weekend." I had never seen him sad when talking about basketball before.

"I can!" I said quickly. "Right, Mom?"

"Sure," she said. And then added, looking at Ernest's

mother, "I'm not going to turn down a night off." She and Ernest's mom and Ernest all laughed.

"I can't wait for tonight," Ernest said. "It'll be the two amigos!"

"The two best amigos," I said.

Jean-Pierre looked morose.

Just then, five Chevys employees came over and formed a half circle around our table. Jennie O'Brien, Fiesta Animal, put a sombrero on Ernest's head.

"What's going on?" Ernest said.

"I told them it's your birthday," I whispered to him. "Just play along—I always do it to my friends here."

They clapped their hands and sang.

Happy, happy birthday
From the Chevys crew!
We wish it was our birthday
So we could party, too!

Everyone in the restaurant applauded for Ernest.

I caught Jean-Pierre's eye and, while nobody else was looking, made a spiral with my index finger like the water-slide in the commercial. He knew what I meant.

*　　*　　*

The sleepover at Ernest's house was a disaster.

". . . and then they put the sombrero on my head and stuff, and they sang this song and stuff, but it was a weird song and not the normal birthday song—"

"I know, Ernest. I was there."

"Do you want anything to drink?" Ernest's mom asked me. We were sitting in the kitchen.

"Sure," I said. "Do you have any soda?"

"Gross!" Ernest said. "Soda gives you cavities."

"How about milk?" I said.

"Ernest is lactose intolerant," said Ernest's mom.

Ernest nodded like that was something to be proud of. "In the mornings I put orange juice in my cereal. That's what we'll have for breakfast tomorrow."

Terrific.

"I'll just have some water."

"What do you want to do?" Ernest asked when we finished our waters.

"Let's watch some TV," I said, since that didn't involve talking to Ernest.

"I can't." Ernest pointed to a poster board filled with boxes on the wall.

"What's that?" I asked.

"Duh, it's my TV Log. Duh," said Ernest. "I can watch

two hours of TV a week. Whenever I watch TV, I mark it on the log. I already used up my time this week."

"Maybe your mom will let you watch some as a treat because I'm here."

"No," called Ernest's mom from the next room.

"Don't worry," Ernest said. "I still have two hours of Nintendo time!"

That was something.

Ernest and I went into the TV room, and he pulled an old video game console out of a cabinet.

"I'm heck of excited about our playdate," Ernest said while he attached the system's wires to the back of the TV.

"Ernest," I said. "I don't think kids our age call them playdates anymore."

"Right," said Ernest, thinking. "Just dates."

"No, playdates is fine."

Ernest turned the TV on and passed me a controller. The title screen was for some fighting game I'd never heard of before. The graphics were terrible.

"This is the first time I've ever used both controllers at once," Ernest said.

For a second, I felt bad for him.

"Winner gets the good controller," said Ernest.

"What do you mean?" I said. A few seconds later I figured

it out. A button on my controller was stuck down and all my character could do was punch the air over and over again.

Ernest started giggling. His character started throwing fireballs at mine. I couldn't dodge them. I lost in about ten seconds.

"I just whupped you," Ernest said. "It's fun to play with two people!"

"Yeah," I said, smiling. "Super fun."

I spent the next hour getting beaten by Ernest at a terrible video game. When Ernest's mom said, "Bedtime!" I almost collapsed with relief. I'd never been so excited to go to sleep at eight thirty p.m.

I stood in Ernest's room. Ernest tossed an old blanket and pillow onto the floor.

The floor was solid wood and covered in dust and toys.

"Am I sleeping on the floor?" I asked.

"Where do you want to sleep?" Ernest asked. "A tree?" He started chuckling.

"It's just I thought you had an extra bed."

"For who? Dracula?" He started laughing again, even harder this time.

"Then why did you tell me I didn't need to bring a sleeping bag?"

"We're not camping!" said Ernest, collapsing in hysterics onto his bed.

I got down on the floor. Ernest turned out his light.

The room was cold and the floor was hard. I didn't know whether to get under the blanket or stay on top of it.

"Do you have any more blankets?" I asked.

"This is a house, not a blanket factory!" Ernest squealed.

I rolled over and tried to find a comfortable position. There wasn't one.

"Want to hear a scary story?" Ernest asked.

"Sure."

"One time there was this driver who picked up this hitchhiker, and the hitchhiker was this girl and she was wearing a prom dress and stuff. . . ."

The girl is a ghost, I thought.

". . . and then they were like talking and stuff, and she was all sad and stuff, and the guy didn't know why . . ."

Because she's a ghost.

". . . and then like when she got to the address. Oh, wait, so first when she originally got in the car, she gave the guy like this address and stuff, and then when they got there, she vanished and stuff. . . ."

Ghost.

". . . and then the guy knocked on the door and stuff,

and this old lady answered, and the guy was like, 'Do you know this girl Donna?' Oh yeah, because originally the guy asked the girl her name, the hitchhiker girl, and her name was Donna, and so the guy was like, 'Do you know this Donna?' And then the woman was like, 'Donna died on prom night and stuff, and so now Donna is like a ghost.'"

"Whoa," I said.

"Yeah, so he gave a ride home to a ghost."

"Right."

That night, when not lying awake with back cramps, I dreamed of Nesquik waterslides.

On Monday morning I was feeling pretty good about my chances of going to the Nesquik factory. I'd heard that Jake Harms had gone over to Ernest's for a sleepover on Saturday night but couldn't take it. At seven thirty he'd faked sick and called his mom.

At morning recess everyone had crowded around Ernest, but he chose to play two square with me.

We sat together at lunch and he told me jokes.

Ernest and I were pretty much the best of friends.

And then, before PE, things took a bad turn.

When I opened the door to the locker room, I saw Ernest in a corner, pushed up against the wall by Hendrick

Samuels. A bunch of boys were crowded around them. Hendrick had a grip on Ernest's gym shirt—a bit of golden cloth was twisted up in his fist.

Hendrick Samuels was two years older than we were, but everyone in our grade knew him because he liked to push smaller kids around. I was usually pretty good at avoiding him.

But as I stood there in the doorway, Ernest looked over at me and we made eye contact. He was helpless. Hendrick looked like a mountain lion that had cornered its prey. He was the size of four or five Ernests put together.

I just wanted to go to my locker and get changed.

But I remembered the waterslide. I pictured myself swirling down the tube and splashing into that pool of chocolate milk. And then I walked over and tapped Hendrick Samuels on the shoulder.

"Come on, Hendrick," I said. "Why are you picking on Ernest? Why don't you pick on someone your own size?"

It wasn't a very good line, but I was using most of my brain to keep my knees from buckling.

Hendrick squinted at me. "He started it. I was getting a drink of water, and this little dork ran up and threw a pair of underwear at me."

I looked over at Ernest, shocked. "You did?"

Ernest giggled and shrugged. "They were clean," he said. Ernest.

If you go around throwing your underwear at Hendrick Samuels, clean or not, you deserved whatever you got.

But the factory.

I stepped between Hendrick and Ernest.

"If you want to mess with Ernest," I said, "you've got to go through me."

Hendrick looked surprised. And amused.

I heard Ernest say behind me, "Thanks, Dean. You're a good friend."

I turned over my shoulder. "You can pay me back by letting me go first on the waterslide."

Ernest hesitated and then said, "Dean? I want to tell you something."

I knew what he'd say: that we were the best of friends.

Ernest whispered in my ear, "There is no sweepstakes. I made that up."

The locker room was quiet, like an empty church. My hands, which had been balled up in fists in front of me, relaxed and dropped to my sides. Oh no. No. My brain pivoted hard. Of course.

Of course Ernest had made it up. If there was a sweepstakes, I would have heard about it, even if my mom wouldn't buy me Nesquik. They would have put that on the commercial.

And Ernest was lactose intolerant. He didn't even drink chocolate milk.

Behind me, I barely heard Ernest say, "I don't even think that factory even exists in real life."

I kept looking straight ahead but I wasn't really seeing. My eyes stung. He was right. Ernest was right. Of course the factory didn't exist. He had known but so many of us had been fooled. How had I missed the truth? It was stupid. You couldn't swim in chocolate milk. That was disgusting. Who would want to drink milk people had swum in? And what if some of the kids hadn't taken showers? And then wouldn't you smell like milk all day? I had fooled myself because I wanted that factory to exist. But now, in a boy's locker room that smelled of chlorine and sweat and the older boys' cologne, the truth hit me hard, right in the gut.

And then Hendrick Samuels did.

WILL
BY ADAM REX

Between peeling off his nightclothes and pulling on his school uniform Will examined himself from heel to hairline. Standing in front of the long mirror with a second, smaller mirror in his hand, he checked every inch of his body for marks, moles, growth, shrinkage, changes in color . . . and made ticks and notes on a long list in his notebook.

If you had read this list you may have found it strange.

Next he pinched himself, held his finger in the flame of a lit match, counted how many jumping jacks he could do in a minute, and timed how long he could hold his breath. When he heard the sound of his older brother moving down the hall Will leaned out the bedroom door and stared at him, squinchy-eyed, until his brother told him to stop.

(This was on the list, too, though you might not have recognized just which item until Will checked it off with a flick of his pencil.)

If you'd been watching through the window you may have thought, at times, that Will was no longer doing anything at all. Just standing there, but with a particularly serious and single-minded look on his face. But each bit of nothing would seem like something when it ended with Will checking another item off his list.

Now he was glaring at a paper clip. What was he trying to do? Was it working? The check mark wouldn't tell you as much as the look on his face or the shake of his head.

Will returned the list with its ticks and checks to his desk drawer, then marked the passing of another day on his wall calendar with a bright red NO. The calendar was nothing but numbers and *nos*.

"Happy Birthday to me," he sighed to himself.

There was a time when Will would have begun the school day by counting his classmates. When their numbers dwindled to about seven he found he didn't need to count anymore—he knew at a glance how many kids remained. Now there were only six, including Will—or there *had* been, at any rate, last Friday.

Four? he thought as he surveyed the room. There were still twenty-five desks in Ms. Chadwick's class but only Aidan, Nathan, and Julie sat there—still in the same seats their last names had determined at the start of the school year but now with vast stretches of empty alphabet between them. *Only four now. That can't be right. . . . Lily and Barry will come in after me*, thought Will, though he was nearly late himself. *Or maybe they're just home sick.*

Will took his seat, said hi to Aidan when Aidan said hi to him, but he never took his eyes off the classroom door. It opened a moment later, but only Ms. Chadwick entered with a really big cup of coffee.

"Quiet down," she said, though no one had been talking. "All stand for the Pledge of Allegiance."

"Where are Lily and Barry?" asked Will without raising his hand.

Ms. Chadwick studied him for a moment, then answered. "Barry found out over the weekend that he's a wizard," she said. "He'll be finishing the year at a wizards' school upstate." Her tone suggested, *always* suggested, that people did not find out they were wizards where she came from. Where *she* came from they might find out they were, say, dentists—but only after a long and tedious period of self-discovery and dental school. "And Lily . . . I have no idea why Lily's gone. How should *I* know?! *I'm* only the teacher!"

She reached with trembling fingers to her lips and felt around for some phantom cigarette she'd probably left in the teachers' lounge. Then she stared at her hand for kind of a long time.

So no Pledge of Allegiance after all. It was just as well. Aidan only pledged his allegiance to Asgard since learning he was the son of Thor, Julie was mute because of some bargain she'd made with a witch or something, and Nathan was a Jehovah's Witness.

"I bet Lily's just sick," Aidan whispered to Will. "There's a flu going around."

Will hadn't heard about any flu, but he nodded and gave Aidan a kind of half-smile. They hadn't really been friends until recently, but of course neither boy had many choices anymore. And Aidan was nice for a demigod. It seemed to Will that you could really let that sort of thing go to your head.

Ms. Chadwick was still staring at her hand.

She was getting that look on her face, that owl look—big fierce eyes and a strong impression that she could turn her head all the way around if she wanted to.

"POP QUIZ!" she hooted. The class groaned, as classes will, but it sounded feeble. There weren't even enough kids to get a good groan going anymore. "An essay, in two hundred words or less! Explain what you think will happen to a teacher if all her students keep turning into flipping butterflies! Assume she has only two years' experience and student loans. Show your work," she added, and went to hide behind her desk for a while. Usually a screaming teacher was like ice down your back, but Ms. Chadwick had been getting gradually louder since Labor Day.

No one, strictly speaking, had actually turned into a butterfly. Hannah had sprouted wings from touching some sort of meteorite back in November, but everyone agreed they were really more dragonfly wings than anything else. She'd done a science fair project about it before leaving for St. Peppermint's Fairy Academy over winter break. Nonetheless, Will took out a sheet of paper and wrote, "What'll Happen to a Teacher If All Her Students Turn into Flipping Butterflies" at the top, and then he thought a moment.

I think if the teacher had our class she wouldn't have to worry. Because the other seventh-grade teacher, Mrs. Murray, is really old and will probably retire and they'll still need someone to teach the seventh grade. And Aidan won't leave because there is no special school for him—he only goes to that Norse god summer camp in Connecticut. Lily's probably just out sick. I don't understand Julie's deal but if she was going to leave she would have left already. And Nathan's too big a loser to get powers.

Will considered that last sentence. Of course he couldn't call his classmate a loser in a school paper. But Nathan had always been a dork. Even more this year than last— he'd turned into one of those kids who raised his hand too much and used words like "however" and "approximately." Still, Will erased a bit and wrote:

And Nathan doesn't seem like the type to be a vampire or leprechaun or whatever. You can just tell with some people.

Then the point of what he'd written sank in a bit and made him feel small.

And you don't have to worry about me, either. I'm never going anywhere. I'll never be a hero or have an adventure. I'll just become a doctor or a banker like my dad or maybe a scientist that finally figures out what's up with this school.

Just then one of the classroom walls collapsed. Aidan gave an exasperated little sigh, because they'd only just finished repairing that wall from the last time.

A chalky cloud of pulverized cinder block settled around the ragged remains, and in stepped a beefy man snapped into some kind of flashy exoskeleton. The brushed-steel limbs of the suit whirred and clicked as he moved, and made his legs two feet taller and arms two feet longer. Chrome tubes and something like a plastic sneeze guard folded over his shoulders and head. Like he was wearing a motorcycle. Will hoped he was maybe just here to talk about Wall Safety, but in his heart he knew the guy was a supervillain. You could just tell with some people.

The supervillain frowned at the class and said, "Is this all of you?"

It seemed like sort of an ordinary question to ask after knocking a wall down. Aidan and Will looked at each other. Nathan scrambled to the other side of the room while Ms. Chadwick ducked behind her desk. Julie, of course, said nothing.

The supervillain tried again. "Where's Lily Landers!?" he roared, in a voice that was sounding more supervillainy until the dust made him cough.

Aha. So Lily was probably a superhero, thought Will. That made sense. She had always been pretty athletic. Maybe her enemies learned her secret identity and she'd gone into hiding. Some kids had all the luck.

"C'mon, guys," the supervillain said. "I know this is her room; the office told me."

He really had been to the office. He had a visitor's badge.

"Lily's absent today," Will offered. "Maybe you could, you know, come back tomorrow."

"Lockdown!" Ms. Chadwick said suddenly, and she popped up from behind her desk with her hands whipping about. "Lockdown! You kids know the drill!"

During Lockdown the school would secure all its doors and gates while the students crouched on the floor with their arms around their heads, and Will felt it was probably something you did *before* the villain punched a hole in the wall. Anyway, Superjerk or whoever blew the door off its hinges with a yellow energy blast from his arm cannon and effectively took the whole question of locking it out of Ms. Chadwick's hands. Slightly singed and whimpering, she crawled back to her desk.

A cool breeze entered through the hole-where-the-door-used-to-be and crossed to the hole-where-the-wall-used-to-be. Outside, teachers and a long line of kids hurried past. The school was being evacuated. Soon Will's class would be all alone with the villain. The police would come, demands would be made. Someone would get hurt.

Will fixed his eyes on Aidan, Son of Thor. *Can you do anything?* he mouthed.

I don't have my hammer, Aidan mouthed back. Will nodded. Their school was a Weapon-Free Zone.

The villain tottered over the ruined wall and stumbled into the classroom. *His suit's impressive, but it isn't all-terrain*, thought Will.

"No moving or talking! Everyone get to the front of the room! We'll wait here until Cheetah Girl hears about it. And comes to save you. Then BOOM! *BOOM!* Why are there only four students?"

"There's a flu going around," said Will as he moved with the other kids to stand in front of the blackboard. He couldn't see any reason not to lie to a supervillain.

"Waitaminute. This is that school."

"What school?"

"You know, *that* school. The one with the kids everyone writes books about."

Will shrugged.

"Wait, I can check," said the villain, and he went a little cross-eyed watching a computer display on the inside of his visor. "I can't . . . I can't seem to connect to your school's wireless. Is there a password?"

"It's 'guest,'" said Ms. Chadwick. She sounded a little shell-shocked.

"Man, it's so slow. I can't even load my home page."

"It might be blocked," said Aidan. "They block a lot of sites."

"Hold on . . . here we go," the villain said. "Oh no." All over his battlesuit flaps and panels opened and shut. "It *is* that school. Can you kids . . . do things?"

Nathan pointed at Aidan. "That boy is super strong."

Will winced. Even without his hammer Aidan was as strong as three men, but the supervillain didn't need to know that. And now he was training his gun on Aidan in a serious way.

"I can read minds," Will said quickly. The other kids looked at him. "Anyone's mind. Yours."

Will saw panic flutter across the man's face, even as he struggled to look unimpressed. Will couldn't read minds, but he'd always been good at reading faces.

"Yeah, prove it. Tell me what I'm thinking right now."

Will squinted. "You're thinking about your greatest weakness."

The villain flinched, and he turned his head, just slightly, just for a moment, to glance at something on his back. "Wait," he said, scowling at Will. "No, I wasn't. That is, I . . . *have* no weakness."

Smooth.

Will examined the suit as best he could. It had clawlike hands and a blaster on each arm. It had a skullcap with earflaps and a chin strap. It had a row of USB ports and a standard electrical outlet on the hip. It had something like a grappling gun between the shoulder blades. Was that what the man was worried about?

"What are we going to do?" whispered Aidan.

"I said no talking!" the villain yelled, and he adjusted some dial by his ear. "I can hear you."

Will had a thought. "Keep whispering," he said as quietly as he could.

"What?" Aidan whispered back.

Superjerk advanced a little, and fiddled with that ear-dial again.

"I can . . . I can hear everything you say," he told them, no longer shouting. "So there's no use whispering."

"Get ready to run," Will whispered, then he kept moving his lips without making any sound at all, just for good measure.

Superjerk took another step forward and turned his

ear-dial all the way up, so that's when Will scratched the blackboard. He'd been growing his nails out anyway, in case he might develop superclaws or something, and the sound of it hurt even him. It made the villain double over as his earflaps rattled and squealed.

The kids all ran through the big hole in the wall to the hallway beyond. Will stole a glance over his shoulder and was relieved to see Ms. Chadwick finally find the presence of mind to flee through the opposite door. Success! Then the villain started firing wildly around the classroom and Will decided to keep moving.

He caught up with the other kids at the front hall of the school, where they heaved at a steel security fence that had been drawn across the exit.

"Oh, man."

"Lockdown!" groaned Aidan as he turned to face Will. "They seriously went and locked all the doors on their way out. We're trapped in here!"

"I can't believe it." Nathan hyperventilated. "I can't believe it."

"Believe it," said Aidan. "Woden's Eye! The teachers here are a bunch of . . . bunch of stupid . . ."

"Stupid, brainless blouse-apes!" Julie wailed as she took a swipe at the fence.

Everyone paused a moment to look at her, and her face flushed.

Then, from around the corner, the sound of servo-motors and footsteps.

"What do we do?" whispered Nathan. "Where do we go?"

The nearest door was the school newspaper office, and they ducked inside and closed it behind them as quietly as they could. Huddled on the floor, they listened to the robotic footfalls of the supervillain pass down the hall. Will's own breathing cut like a saw blade through his chest, and he could think of nothing but coughing, but soon the hallway sounds faded away.

Aidan flipped a wall switch and the ceiling lights flickered on. The newspaper room was filled with dusty computers and magazines. A few small silver cameras were still connected to laptops by black USB cords, as if abandoned in the middle of a project. The newspaper didn't have a big circulation anymore.

"It's my birthday today," Will whispered to no one in particular.

"Wow," said Aidan. "Crappy birthday."

"I know."

"So that means . . ."

Will knew what it meant. There wasn't any rule that said the Big Change had to come before a person turned thirteen, but almost everyone at his school got it when they were eleven or twelve or they never got it at all.

"Don't you have an older brother?" asked Aidan. "He's got some power or something, right?"

When Will's brother was in the fifth grade he and a couple friends discovered a magic tree house that could travel through time, and had taken it on all kinds of funny adventures. But in high school they'd lost interest in time travel, and it mostly became a magical place to smoke. Until they accidentally burned it down last August. And they'd never let Will use it anyway.

"No," said Will.

"Wait," said Nathan. "So you lied about reading minds?"

"Yeah."

"But you got him to think about his greatest weakness," Julie said quietly. "And he looked at his back."

"I know. What do you think he's worried about?"

"I don't mean to be rude," said Nathan, "but that man doesn't seem smart enough to have built his suit himself. It looks an awful lot like an experimental project that Hannibal Tech has been working on for the military. This fellow probably stole one of the prototypes."

All of them had stopped what they were doing to look at Nathan. Aidan asked, "How do you know all that stuff?"

"I'm not really Nathan. I'm his father, Mr. Peterson. Nate and I switched bodies accidentally over the summer."

"How'd that happen?"

"Wished on the same penny."

"We should stay focused on the suit," said Will. "Mr. Peterson, do you work for Hannibal or something?"

"That's right. Or I did, before the switch. Now Nate works there."

"What can you tell us about that exoskeleton?"

Mr. Peterson looked startled. Specifically, he looked like Nathan looking startled. "Oh, gosh . . . not much. I can tell you it costs eight point three million dollars. I'm only an accountant."

"Nothing else?"

"Um . . . it's powered by fusion or antimatter or something. And we're trying to save money, so it just runs Windows."

This gave Will an idea, and he pocketed one of the cameras. Its cord hung like a tail from the back of his jeans.

There came then the distant sound of the villain's energy blast, and the muffled collapse of another wall. The kids all tensed. Then it all happened again, but louder. Closer.

Then the east wall of the school newspaper office split open and crumbled into the room.

"Go! Go!" Will shouted as he pushed everyone else toward the door. Again the supervillain came doddering like a drunk over the chunky debris.

"What now?!" said Aidan.

Will tried to remember which classrooms had doors to the outside. "Science room!" he answered with a frown. He was never going to get a good look at the back of that battlesuit if they were always running away.

They raced down the hall as the sound of more blasts echoed off the linoleum. "YOU KIDS!" the villain's voice boomed. The suit apparently had a PA system. "STOP MAKING THIS SO DIFFICULT!"

Seconds later they spread out across the science classroom. Aidan pulled at the courtyard door with his mighty strength, but he only managed to rip off the handle. Will and the others searched the workstations and cabinets for something they could use against the villain.

"So . . . you can talk," Will said to Julie when she came near.

Julie blushed again, and smiled, and covered the smile with her hand. "Yes."

"So that whole story about the witch's curse?"

She looked away. "I made it up. I just don't like talking in class."

"So . . . you don't have any special . . . powers? Things, whatever? Like me?"

Julie shrugged. Will smiled at her, and she smiled back, then blushed harder and turned abruptly to search the supply closet.

"We could turn on all the gas jets," said Mr. Peterson from the center of the room. Each workstation had a natural gas valve for fueling Bunsen burners. "Fill the room with gas. Then when that . . . criminal fires his weapon . . ."

"We all blow up," Aidan finished.

"We could be out of the room."

"So what would he be shooting at if we're not in the room?"

"Maybe he'll want to blow another hole in a wall. He's always doing that. Look: I'm the adult here—"

"I wonder . . ." Will said absently. After a moment he noticed the room had fallen silent and all eyes were on him.

"What?" said Aidan.

"Just . . . you notice when Superjerk comes through a wall he gets real shaky and nervous stepping over the rubble? Like he's afraid he'll fall over."

"Yeah? So?"

"So his greatest weakness . . . I don't think it's *on* his back, I think it *is* his back. I think if he falls on his back he can't get up again."

Mr. Peterson was nodding slowly. "Yeah. Yeah, that makes sense. Nate told me just the other night that R & D wants more money to give the battlesuit something called a 'hydraulic back-a-pult.' I told him to deny the request—they're way over budget."

"But how do we get him on his back?" asked Julie.

"God-boy can push him," said Mr. Peterson. "He's strong."

"Yeah, and Superjerk *knows* he's strong," Will answered, glaring. "*Some*one told him. He's not going to let Aidan get within five feet of him before he starts blasting. Aidan, are you invulnerable or anything?"

"Not until I'm older."

"See? So, no, Aidan can't just rush him. Look, I have an idea, but if it doesn't—"

Will never got a chance to explain his idea. From the hall door came a metallic squeak, and then the door was wrenched free of its hinges. The villain tossed it aside like garbage and the kids each ducked behind the closest workstation. Will peeked around the edge.

"Look, guys . . ." the villain said. He tried to step through the opening he'd made, couldn't, then turned sideways and crab-walked into the room. "I don't want to shoot a bunch of kids—even the supervillain community frowns on that kind of thing—but I will if you don't cooperate. Just line up where I can see you, and when Cheetah Girl gets here I'll kill her and leave."

He punctuated this last statement with a few energy blasts to the science room equipment cabinet. Pressboard doors splintered and Pyrex petri dishes shattered, musically.

"Why do you want to kill her?" called Will. Anything to keep the man talking instead of shooting things. "Are you her arch nemesis or something?

"Oh, man, I wish. She probably hasn't even heard of me yet, honestly—I'm kind of an up-and-comer. But word's gotten around about her secret identity, and I've never defeated a superhero, so . . . It's really the only reason I haven't made it to the big time."

"What's your name?" shouted Aidan.

The villain fired off a couple rounds at the ceiling. "I AM CALLED . . . CYBERSTRUCTO!"

Will could suddenly think of another reason why this guy had never made the big time.

"Okay. Cyberstructo? I'm going to come out," said Will, and he rose slowly from his hiding place, hands in the air.

"It's me, the boy who can read minds, except I can't really, that was a lie, I can't do anything, I was trying to make you reveal your weakness but you don't have one, so . . ."

He'd watched a lot of action movies and nobody ever seemed to die right in the middle of a sentence, so he tried to make each thought sort of blend into the next.

". . . so you can have me, 'cause you don't need all of us and you can just let the other kids go, all right?"

He was getting closer, getting *CLOSER* to the evil robot man with the guns, and each step was harder and heavier. Shards of Pyrex crunched beneath his sneakers, and the villain was smiling.

"That's right," Cyberstructo said in a tone of voice he'd probably picked up from some kids' show about feelings. "I only need one of you. Come closer."

Will came closer.

Cyberstructo seized the scruff of his sweater in his metal claw and hoisted Will three feet in the air. The hot barrel of the villain's arm cannon creased the back of Will's skull.

"Oh, man." Cyberstructo chuckled. "Too easy. I hope Cheetah Girl is this stupid. Okay, you kids. Everybody up, everybody to the front of the room or I blow his head off."

Will had only seconds. The other kids (and Mr. Peterson) were already beginning to rise, to give themselves away. He fished around behind him, groping at the empty air for—yes, there it was. The camera cord. The thin plastic of it bumped against his palm and he closed his fingers, slid them down the length of it until he found the end.

"You know," said Cyberstructo, "I should probably kill at least one of you or it'll look bad. Like I'm too soft. Then maybe you'll behave—"

Will pinwheeled around and plugged the camera cord into a USB port on Cyberstructo's hip. The villain went stiff.

"What's happened!? I can't move. I can't move, and now all I see are pictures of a tetherball game."

"Aidan!" shouted Will. "Now!"

Aidan started, then rushed forward and sacked the quarterback. Cyberstructo rose an inch in the air and came down hard on his back. So did Will.

"Ow."

"You okay?" said Aidan, ripping Will free of the villain's claw and ruining a perfectly good sweater.

"I'm fine," Will answered. He had a sore head and a sick taste in his mouth, but he didn't want to be a whiner.

"AAAH! No!" said Cyberstructo. He regained control of his arms and legs and flailed them like a fussy baby.

"Better stay out of his way," said Will. "He can probably shoot that gun again if he wants to."

"What did you do to him?" asked Mr. Peterson.

"Well . . . that suit of his—it's just a big computer, right? And I don't know a computer that doesn't drop everything when you plug a camera into it."

"YOU STUPID KIDS!"

Cyberstructo wiggled and rattled, whirred and clicked, but he wasn't going anywhere. He fired in frustration at the pressboard ceiling.

"HELP ME UP SO I CAN KILL YOU!"

"Auto-destruct sequence engaged," said a new voice, a female voice from somewhere deep in Cyberstructo's circuitry.

"What did that say?" said Cyberstructo.

"What did that say?" said Aidan.

"Antimatter core will detonate in fifteen seconds."

"A self-destruct," Mr. Peterson whispered. "So if it falls on its back it won't fall into enemy hands."

"Did you know about this?!" Aidan demanded.

"There was . . . there was a line item on a budget request but I didn't—"

"Shut up!" said Julie. "What do we do? Run?"

"Ten seconds."

"No!" Cyberstructo pleaded. "Don't leave me!"

"We could never run far enough."

A shutter opened to reveal a cavity in Cyberstructo's breastplate, and a bright, jittering yellow sphere of antimatter the size of a Ping-Pong ball. It crackled with power.

Aidan and Mr. Peterson looked to Will, waiting to be told what to do. Julie's eyes were on the antimatter.

"FIVE SECONDS."

Will hadn't a thought in his head.

Julie pounced on the battlesuit, scooped out the antimatter ("Ooh, hot."), and popped it in her mouth. She swallowed it like it was a dry aspirin and grimaced as it fizzled and died inside her.

There was a moment of utter quiet. Then she shot the other kids a guilty look.

"Okay, I'm an alien. Please don't tell my mom I told."

Cheetah Girl arrived a few minutes later. She was on the scene in a flash with her superspeed, buzzing around the room, trying to assess the situation. Only when the other kids convinced her it was all over did she finally stand still.

She was wearing her golden costume and mask, of course, but it was obviously Lily. Will couldn't believe he'd never guessed it before.

Aidan explained everything that had happened and they

all had a laugh, though when he called her Lily instead of Cheetah Girl she launched into a big "Lily? Who is this Lily you speak of" routine so the conversation ended kind of awkwardly. Then the news reporters started closing in, and Cheetah Girl looked anxious to leave. On the evening news they would get the whole story wrong and claim *she* had saved the day instead of Aidan, but that wasn't her fault. By the time the reporters got near enough to hurl their questions, Cheetah Girl was gone.

Will and Aidan watched her disappear, just a yellow blur on the horizon.

"Sucks about you not getting powers," said Aidan.

"I know." Will sighed. "I'll never be a hero."

ARTEMIS BEGINS
BY EOIN COLFER

I have four brothers. That's five boys altogether all living in a small house, which is a recipe for major property damage at the very least. As kids, each of us had our assigned roles in the family, pretty much like the members of boy bands do today. Paul, the eldest, was the wise and reliable one. I was the aspiring writer, bespectacled and be-notebooked. Eamonn was the tearaway, never without a nest of twigs in his hair and a bleeding cut on his knee. Niall was the cutie-pie blond baby. But the brother with the most interesting role, as far as an aspiring writer was concerned, was brother number three: Donal. Donal was the young criminal mastermind.

Donal has always been the fixer in our house. If someone was in trouble, Donal could get them out of it, especially if the someone in trouble was himself and the trouble was of the kind visited on a little boy by his angry mother when the boy had totally smashed something he had been expressly forbidden to touch on pain of death or at the very least no TV for a week. Donal was always touching those kinds of things and often smashing them into more pieces than there were of Humpty Dumpty post–wall tumble. (What was an egg doing perched on a wall anyway? And why would all the king's horses be so upset about one egg? It all sounds suspiciously like forced rhyming to me.) Donal's tried-and-true method for getting out of trouble was to use the fact that our mother liked him quite a bit; in fact, it could be said that she loved him lots then and still does today in spite of all the mayhem he caused in the 1980s.

Donal callously played on this love to escape punishment. Even from a young age, his method was infallible: blink in a cute, babylike fashion and declare in a babylike voice how much he "wuves his mommy." The key element in his whole scam was the aforementioned babylike-ishness, which cleverly transported my mother back to the day when Donal was a mere baby who could do no wrong, when the summers were longer and the music charts were full of actual songs that a person could sing along to.

And so no matter what Donal had been caught doing,

he invariably got off with a mild tousling of the hair and perhaps, in extreme cases, a little finger waggling, which really ticked off the rest of us, who had to bear real punishments when we were caught doing anything wrong. But as much as we resented Donal's untouchable status, we also admired him a little bit. After all, what mother's son wouldn't like to be able to gurn his way out of trouble whenever it suited him?

As Donal grew, so did his experience and the intricacies of his plans to avoid punishment. And it wasn't long before we started turning to Donal in times of trouble to see if he could work some of his magic for us. Obviously we were prepared to pay. That went without saying. Donal was a payment-orientated kind of guy from a very early age who wouldn't tie a toddler's shoelace for less than a bag of gummi bears. So we went to him bearing gifts of potato chips or Wham bars or space poppers and begged him for a strategy to dig us out of the hole we were in. Once I scratched the door of Dad's car with my bike handle. The car was only secondhand, which was the equivalent of brand-new for us, and I knew I was for the high jump. (This is a metaphor. We didn't have an actual Olympic high jump in our garden. The official run-up track alone would have to be twenty meters long. Where do you think we lived, Buckingham Palace?) Donal took a look and gave me a bottle of Mom's nail varnish to cover the scratch. It was a close enough match, and I was in university before dad noticed the camouflage. This little favor cost me more than candy. In payment, Donal forced me to call him by the title Sir Donal, Prince of Goodness, for an entire month.

This went on for a few years, and Donal got a bit of a reputation as the neighborhood fixer. Kids came from blocks away to hear his wisdom. They came with bonbons in their wagons and left with favors, tricks, con jobs, and sob stories. But Donal's pièce de résistance, the one that the kids still talk about in the school yard, was pulled off in our own house with our own baby brother.

It happened like this. Every parent has to have an interest to stop their children turning them into blubbering head cases who sit in corners sucking their thumbs and flipping through photos of times when they were happy. In my mother's case this interest was amateur dramatics.

She was the Wexford Drama Group's leading actress. She played everything from a Southern belle to a society heiress. And one year, for her portrayal of an eighteenth-century island girl, my mother brought home the award for All-Ireland Best Actress. This was a proud moment for the Colfer family.

We were shown the crystal plate engraved with my mother's name; we were even allowed to run our fingers along the carved facets and watch the light refracted along its edges. Then the plate was placed in our display case and we were warned never to touch it again. A warning like this pretty much ensures that the plate would be touched often and inevitably broken by one of the brood.

My baby brother, Niall, was the unfortunate who was destined to become the breaker. It could have been any one of us, as we regularly took down the plate when my mother was occupied. We used it to do crayon rubbings; we rolled its edges through uncooked pastry. It made a very effective puck in table hockey, and of course if a person felt like balancing something on his forehead, the award plate was the perfect size.

It was the table hockey that was to be Niall's downfall. As the youngest in the family, he was a little short for the table and had never actually won a game, and so he decided to get in a little solo practice. It was only when he had struck the plate a square whack and it was skittering toward the other end of the table that it dawned on his pea brain that if there was no one at the receiving end, then the plate would fly off and, presuming gravity didn't suddenly fail, crash to the ground.

Gravity did not fail, and my mom's All-Ireland Best Actress crystal plate fell to the tiled floor and smashed into a thousand rainbow pieces. Three pieces and he might have been able to jigsaw them back together and it could have been days before Mom noticed. But a thousand? His goose was cooked.

There was only one person to turn to. Niall rushed into the garden where Donal was burying our neighbor's G.I. Joe so he could blackmail him for his pocket money later. I, in my role as budding writer, was observing and taking notes.

We knew Niall was in trouble when we saw him coming. He had not done his hair, and Niall always did his hair before venturing outside. He was very vain about his blond mop, still is. And there were twin streams of mucus streaming from his nose, which either meant that he had eaten pepper again or that he had been crying.

"Donal! Eoin!" he cried. "Help! Help!"

I waved my hand across my face, Obi-Wan style. "I am not here," I said.

Niall was six, so this did not compute. "Huh?"

"I am not here," I repeated, jiggling my head for effect.

Niall's mucus glands went into panicked overdrive. "Eoin is dead!" he wailed at Donal. "And his ghost is sitting on the grass right there."

"Eoin is being a writer," said Donal, and Niall instantly calmed, as everybody knows that writers do stupid things all the time.

Niall's calm evaporated when he remembered his own crisis. "I broke Mum's award. She'll be back in a minute."

Mum was in the front garden chatting to our neighbor. Niall had mere moments before she stepped inside to find her beloved plate shattered.

"You broke the award," said Donal, who did not seem too upset; in fact, he seemed delighted that someone else was in trouble for a change.

"Yes. I broke the award."

As I was taking notes I decided that I would edit this conversation, as it was getting a bit repetitive.

"Who broke the award?" asked Donal, dragging it out.

Niall pointed to his own head. "It was me. I broke the award."

Donal mashed a clod of clay onto G.I. Joe's head. "Well, if you're the one who broke Mum's award, you might as well leave home now, because she's going to go straight to DEFCON four."

Donal loved using military terms to confuse his little brother.

"DEFCON four?"

"Oh, yep. I remember a milkman made the wrong delivery once. Gave Mom a bit of cheek, and she went from zero to DEFCON four in six point three seconds. Broke every bottle of milk in the lorry. Stamped on all the yogurt cartons. It was a massacre."

This was good stuff. I wrote as quickly as I could. Donal was a gold mine.

Niall's face fell. "A massacre?"

He was a clever boy. Only six years old and already he knew what the word "massacre" meant. He tugged on Donal's mucky sleeve. "You can help me, Donnie. You know stuff. Everyone in the estates knows you have powers."

Donal was torn. On the one hand there is nothing a big brother likes better than seeing his little brother up to his neck in trouble, especially when that little brother is such a cutie that trouble usually slides off him. But on the other hand his professional curiosity was aroused. Could he get Niall off the hook for such an extreme crime? If he managed it, the name Donal would become legendary around the estates.

I could be bigger than Santa Claus, I imagined him imagining.

Eventually Donal thought of a plan that could both dig Niall out of the hole he was in and inflict a little brotherly pain at the same time. Perfect.

"I will help you," he said magnanimously.

"Thanks, brother," said Niall, collapsing in a grateful heap. "He's great, isn't he, Eoin?"

"I am not here, remember?" I said. Some people are a bit slow to catch on.

Donal brought Niall to the top of the stairs, where they waited for my mother's return. I followed a couple of spaces behind. I had an idea what was coming but it would have been wrong of me to intervene, just as it would be wrong of a nature reporter to come between two monkeys in the wild.

"When Mom sees the smashed award she will be furious," Donal explained.

Niall nodded. "DEFCON four."

"Exactly, grasshopper. So, my job is to somehow turn that fury into sympathy. I have to do something so extreme that Mom won't even remember why she was angry in the first place."

Niall was nodding like a little bobblehead toy. He would have done anything. Anything.

"All you have to do is kneel here, at the edge of the stairs, and when I give the signal, scream like you're in great pain."

"What's the signal?" asked Niall, which I thought was a fair question, but Donal would not have agreed with my thought had I voiced it, which I didn't, as I was merely an observer.

"What's the signal?" Donal repeated, shocked. "What's the sig . . . Are you questioning my methods? Are you trying to run the show? Maybe I should just leave you to get out of trouble yourself and see how far you get."

Niall's nose candles dripped in shock. "No. No. Don't go. I'll be good."

"You will be obedient," corrected Donal. "Like a puppy!"

"Woof," said Niall.

"Okay. You'll know the signal when you see it." Donal poked his head between the banister posts. "Now we wait."

It was not a long wait. Mere seconds later we heard the familiar snick of the front door closing and the mutter of Mom's voice as she complained to herself about the person she had just been talking to. We followed her footsteps down the hallway and into the kitchen, where the crystal shards would be winking a Morse code of guilt that read: NIALL NIALL NIALL.

"Niall!" my mother shrieked, being well-versed in crystal codes. "Niall!"

"Here we go," said Donal, rubbing his hands.

Niall pointed at the rubbing hands. Was that the signal? He was afraid to ask.

Mom was on the hunt now. She picked up the trail of muddy trainers coming in the back door, followed it to the bottom of the stairway. From above, her body language seemed a little hostile. An impression that was not helped by the wringing of a dishcloth between her fingers.

"Mom is wishing that was your neck," said Donal to Niall with a merry wink.

"Niall," called Mom. "Niall!"

Her eyes swept up the stairs, following the trail of mud, and just before her gaze rested on the culprit, Donal decided that it was time for the signal.

In one violent motion, Donal elbowed Niall off the top step and sent him tumbling down the stairs.

"Scream, grasshopper," he called after his rapidly descending brother. "Scream your little lungs out."

Niall did not need to be told twice; in fact he didn't need to be told once. He screamed with great gusto and in genuine fright, pausing only to take a mouthful of carpet at every revolution. Down and down he went, making a xylophone of the banister posts with his legs, bashing the air from his lungs. And when he finally came to rest at my mother's feet, the fury was whipped from her face like a tissue in the wind and replaced by maternal concern.

"My baby!" she cried, sinking to her knees, cradling Niall's head, the broken award utterly forgotten. "My baaaaby!"

On the top step, Donal surveyed the scene with some satisfaction. He had, he knew, saved Niall's hide while simultaneously securing his place in local legend.

He shot a salute down to his bleeding baby brother and whispered, "You're welcome."

Donal actually patted himself on the back, then turned to me and said, "Did you get that, writer gimp? I am the biggest genius wot you shall ever meet. You should do a book about me."

I could only stare in awe. There was no doubt that he was an evil genius, but likable, too. A curious mixture. Surely people would like to read about a boy like this.

And the seeds for the Artemis Fowl series were sewn.

The following day, Mom remembered the broken award, and Niall was grounded with no TV for a month. Donal never mentions that part.

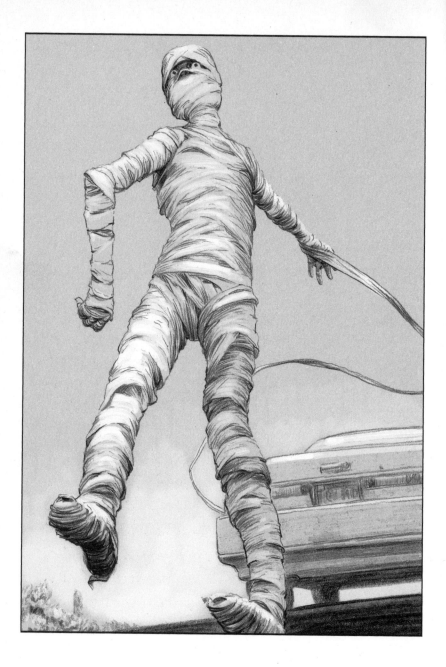

KID APPEAL
BY DAVID LUBAR

Dwight Howtzler is an idiot. He's also my best friend. Brains aren't all that important most of the time, and they're definitely not the first thing I look for when I pick my friends. For example, Zeke Walther, that motormouth show-off, is super smart, but I'd never want to hang out with him.

There are lots of other things that make someone a great best friend, like loyalty and courage. Dwight's totally loyal. He'd never tell on me, no matter what I did. Even though he got six weeks of detention, Dwight never admitted he had help when he dumped twenty packs of cherry Kool-Aid into the school's new fishpond. I swear we thought there weren't any fish in it yet. I guess it's a good thing only two of them were hiding in there at the time. They looked real pretty right before they turned belly up. It was sort of like a Dr. Seuss story. One fish, two fish. Red fish, dead fish.

And to this day, nobody who could punish me for it has a clue I was with Dwight when we snuck into the principal's office and replaced the regular CD of the National Anthem with one where the whole song was burped. At least he got only one week of detention for that.

As for courage, I know Dwight would stand right next to me if I got attacked by a band of ninjas or a pack of zombies. If I got bitten by a snake, I'd bet he'd even suck out the poison. As long as I got bitten on the leg or arm. If I got bitten on the butt, I'd understand if he let me die.

So being smart isn't important most of the time. But it's sort of helpful when you're entering a contest. And it looked like we'd be doing that. You see, right before the last bell, our teacher, Ms. Flayer, handed out a bunch of papers, like she does every Friday. It was the usual stuff: a bake sale, eye exams, a book fair, something about a sewage leak in the cafeteria. Nothing important.

When she got back to her desk, she waved a sheet of yellow paper at us. "I hope some of you will consider entering this contest."

Contest? I loved winning stuff. I shuffled through the papers and found the yellow one. I got as far as the first line: CELEBRATE THE HISTORY OF NEW CAIRO.

I stopped right there. I'd rather celebrate the fact that my gum lasted for three hours this morning. Our teachers had been jamming the town's history down our throats since way back in first grade. After five years of that, New Cairo's past was the last thing I wanted to celebrate.

I guess Dwight read the whole paper, because he grabbed my arm as soon as we got into the hall and said, "We are so doing this, Charlie. It's going to be awesome."

"Doing what?" I pulled my arm free, which wasn't easy since Dwight is one of the biggest kids in our class.

"Look at this!" He shoved the paper in my face and pointed at the next line. WIN BIG PRIZES!!!!!

Okay—that caught my attention. But I knew "big prizes" meant different things to adults than it did to kids. Grown-ups actually seemed to think a kid would get all excited about a savings bond or a dictionary. Anything that's going to get my heart racing needs to say stuff like "radio controlled" and "Wi-Fi enabled."

But I guess, once in a while, an adult gets it right. According to the flyer, first prize was a trip for two to the grand opening of Splashtastic Park. I'd heard it had fifteen water slides and a gigantic saltwater wave pool, all inside a dome. That would be a perfect way to start summer vacation, which was only two weeks away. I'd been dying to go there ever since I'd seen the ads, but my parents said it was too expensive.

Suddenly, the history of New Cairo sounded a lot more interesting. I read the rest of the flyer. It turned out the New Cairo Chamber of Commerce—whatever that was— was sponsoring the contest to help celebrate the 150th anniversary of the town's founding.

"We have a week," I said after I read the rules. The projects had to be brought to school next Friday and set up in the auditorium. The whole school would have an assembly at the end of the day to watch the judging.

"That's tons of time," Dwight said. "I do most of my projects the day before they're due. Or even that morning. And I've never gotten lower than a C minus. Except once or twice."

"I think, if we're gonna do it, we better give it a bit more time than just one day."

"If?" Dwight asked.

"I've got a ton of math and reading to slog through." I glanced back at our classroom door. Ms. Flayer seemed to think that homework kept kids from getting into trouble.

If that was true, I never would have tried to make grilled cheese sandwiches for me and Dwight using his mom's iron or jump my bicycle from the garage roof to the porch last week. I was still picking scabs off my knee from the crash. But that's okay—I sort of like picking scabs.

"We have to do it," Dwight said. "It's our only chance to get to the Splashtastic Park grand opening. I've heard it's going to be awesome."

"I don't know. . . ."

That's when a high-pitched laugh shattered my thoughts. It sounded like someone was tickling a gigantic baby with a pitchfork.

"You guys are going to enter?" Zeke Walther, who'd slithered up behind us, cackled again, then said, "Forget it. Unless they add a nice last-place prize. There's no way you losers have a chance. Not against me. I'm full of smarts. You're just full of farts." He smirked and walked off.

I turned to Dwight, held up my hand, and said, "Let's do it."

He smacked my palm. "We'll show him who the loser is. I can already feel myself floating in that wave pool." He closed his eyes and swayed from side to side like he was up to his neck in the water. Then he farted.

"Dwight! Knock it off."

"Sorry," he said. "I like making bubbles."

"You're not in a real pool," I said.

"Good point."

I reminded myself not to get too close to him once we hit the water. And we were definitely hitting that water. Somehow, some way, my idiot friend and I were going to win first prize. Whatever we did, I had a feeling I'd be doing all of the thinking and most of the work. That didn't stop Dwight from spitting out a stream of ideas as we walked to my place.

"We could bring in cookies," he said. "I could get my mom to bake them. Everyone loves her cookies."

"It's supposed to be about something from the history of the town," I said. "Cookies don't count."

"What if she makes them now and we let them get stale? Then they'd be historic. And she lives here, so they'd be from the town." He grinned at me. "Wow. I thought this would be harder."

"It still won't count," I said. "Even if it did, we need to come up with something way better than cookies."

"Oh." Dwight sighed, stared at the ground for a moment, then let out a whoop and clapped his hands together. "I got it! This is perfect! We'll make one of those diarrhea things."

"What are you talking about?" My brain wrestled with

itself, trying to think up any possible connection between stomach cramps and history.

"You know, a shoebox diarrhea," Dwight said. "Where you cut out stuff, color it, and glue it in the box."

"That's a diorama," I said. "Not a diarrhea." Now my brain was wrestling with the image of Dwight carrying a sloshing shoebox to school. Luckily my imagination was nice enough to make sure the box had a lid on it.

"Diorama?" he asked. "You sure?"

"Yup. I'm positive."

"Shoot. I guess that explains why Mrs. Esheritchia kept laughing at me last year when I turned in my project and told her it was the best diarrhea I'd ever made." Dwight stared at the ground for another minute as we walked. "So, anyhow, you think we should make one of those?"

"Half the kids who enter are going to do that," I said. "The other half will probably do some sort of poster."

"What about the third half?" Dwight asked.

"That would be us," I said. "We need to come up with something awesome. We have to completely blow away all the shoeboxes and posters."

By the time we reached my house, Dwight had tossed out a bunch more suggestions—most of which had nothing to do with history. The couple things that might have worked would also definitely get both of us expelled if we brought them to school. Though I had to admit that the idea of making a full-size, fully working Civil War cannon was sort of cool. So was an authentic Samurai sword, even though I didn't think there was any connection between Japanese warriors and New Cairo.

A blast of freezing cold air hit us as we went inside. Dad must have been trying to use the thermostat again. Last year, to save energy, Dad bought this fancy electronic thermostat with programmable timers that controlled the heat and air-conditioning in all the rooms in the house. But he still didn't understand how to set it, so I never knew whether I'd be coming home to a refrigerator or an oven, or some combination of freezing and steaming rooms. The main control panel was in the hallway, right by the stairs. I switched off the air-conditioning and turned on some heat so the house would warm up quickly.

We went into the living room to watch TV and kick around ideas. My parents both worked, but Mom had left a snack for me.

"Whoa, that's huge." Dwight grabbed the half-gallon jar of crunchy peanut butter from the coffee table.

"Yeah. Mom's been shopping at that new warehouse place, Big Globs. Last week, she bought a ten-pound bag of Fig Newtons." I opened the box of crackers. It looked like there were enough to shingle a roof.

After we got settled, I started searching for something to watch. There was a science program playing high up past the channels where they show all the infomercials. A couple guys in a museum were examining mummies.

"That's it!" Dwight shouted. "We'll make you into a mummy."

"That's crazy." I looked at the front of his shirt. "And don't shout when your mouth is full of crackers." It's a good thing my folks own a really good vacuum cleaner.

Dwight brushed off the crumbs. "But that's how the town got its name. Right?"

"Yeah, that's true. . . ." From what we'd learned at school, right around the time of the Civil War this guy named Joshua Stirling traveled around the southwest, charging people money to see an authentic Egyptian mummy taken from a secret tomb in Cairo. When his wagon broke down near the Skenbatch Creek, he decided to stay there.

He built a little cabin and turned it into a sort of museum where people could come and see the mummy. And for a while, people did. But there weren't a lot of people living around there at the time, so eventually everyone had seen it. Joshua Stirling could have moved on, but he liked where he was. So he tried something different. He started grinding up bits of the mummy to sell to people as medicine.

I guess people were pretty stupid back then, because Joshua Stirling made a ton of money with his mummy powder. He started selling other cures and remedies. After a while, he ran out of mummy, but by then he had a small store that sold all kinds of medicine, some of which actually made people better, or at least didn't make them sicker. That's how New Cairo began. A couple other companies also started making medicine here, and then, about thirty years ago, they built a medical school and a hospital. Now the school and the hospital are among the best in the country.

Despite all of this, I didn't think that dressing me up as a mummy was going to get us any prizes. I put down the remote. "Let's get serious. How are we going to win this thing?"

"I know you said we can't use cookies for our project. But what if we gave cookies to the judges?"

Dwight's suggestion, as stupid as it was, actually gave me an idea. "We can't bribe the judges. But we can appeal to them."

"Peel them?" Dwight frowned. "They aren't going to let us do that."

"No. *Appeal* to them. We can make sure our project is

something that they especially like. Hang on."

I dug the flyer out of my backpack. The sponsors were listed at the bottom of the sheet: Kendra's Chocolate Cottage, Delancy's Butcher Shop, and Mitchell's Sporting Goods. "Okay, so we need a project that people who are into chocolate, meat, and sports will like." This was good. I'd bet Zeke wouldn't think of aiming at the judges.

"We could play catch with chocolate-covered meatballs. All the judges would love that." Dwight flashed me a grin, then he frowned and said, "Wait. Maybe it's a bad idea."

"I'm glad you figured that out all by yourself."

"Yeah. If they're chocolate covered, nobody would know there's meat inside." He scratched his head. "This could be tricky."

"At least we know what kind of idea we need to find."

"That's a good start." Dwight picked up the remote and switched channels. "Hey, look. Martians with chain saws. Cool. They have four arms."

"Whoa," I said as the scene got violent. "Make that three arms."

"This is great. I can't believe your parents don't block this channel."

"They don't know how." Like with the thermostat, my parents were clueless about technology. If they ever figured out how to use any of the electronics in our house, my life wouldn't be anywhere near as nice.

At least the room was finally comfortable. I went back to the control panel and switched off the heat so it wouldn't get too hot. My folks had also spent big bucks getting new windows and extra insulation for the house last year. We sat back and watched the rest of the movie. By the time it ended, Dwight had to go home.

"We'll figure the rest out next week," I said. There was no way I was doing any extra thinking on the weekend. "At least we know what we're doing."

"We're going to win for sure," Dwight said.

I met up with him outside of school on Monday morning. Before we could talk about our project, Zeke strutted up to us and said, "You guys might as well quit right now. My project is going to be unbeatable."

"Doesn't matter what you do," Dwight said. "You're going to lose, because we—"

"Have a better one," I said, before Dwight could say something stupid like *We're going to appeal to the judges.* I didn't want anyone to steal our plan.

"Yeah, right," Zeke said. "And I'm going to grow wings and fly around the school. Forget it. You're going to lose."

"Wanna bet?" Dwight said.

"How much?" Zeke asked.

Dwight turned toward me. "I have twenty dollars left from my birthday."

"I can match that," I said. It would wipe out my savings if I lost, but we had a great plan, and it would be wonderful to make Zeke a double loser.

"All right, then. We'll bet thirty bucks," Dwight said.

"Forty," I whispered to him.

"Forty," he said.

"You've got a bet," Zeke said. "This is going to be awesome. A trip to Splashtastic Park and lots of spending money. I can't wait to beat you losers."

He barked out his annoying laugh again and walked off.

"We'd better win," I said.

"We can't lose," Dwight said. "We have a plan. We just need to work out the details."

He was right. It wouldn't be that hard to come up with something now that we had a strategy.

"Ready to get to work?" I asked Dwight when we left school at the end of the day.

"Absolutely. We are totally going to make an awesome project."

We headed toward my house. A block later, Dwight stopped walking and spun toward Main Street. "Wait. We need to go into town first."

"Why?"

"The new issue of *Zombie Ghost Pirates* comes out today."

"The one where they fight the werewolf motorcycle gang?" I asked.

"That's the one."

"Then we definitely have to go into town." I couldn't believe a whole month had passed since the last issue had come out.

We headed off for the comic book store. There was a lot of other cool stuff to look at. "We still have tons of time for the project," I said when we finally left the store.

"For sure," Dwight said. "Tons."

The comic was awesome. So was the movie we stumbled across the next day.

"It shouldn't be this hard," Dwight said on Wednesday.

"Maybe we're making it hard," I said as I fiddled with the thermostat again. No matter how long we'd spent thinking and talking, we'd totally failed to come up with something that all three judges would like. That's when it hit me. "Hey—we don't need to get all three judges to like us. Just two of them would be enough for us to win."

Dwight stared at me. "But there are three judges."

"Trust me," I said. "If we get two votes, we win."

"Which two?" he asked.

"Doesn't matter. Whichever are the easiest. Let's see. . . ." I thought about the combinations. "There's meat and chocolate, meat and sports, or sports and chocolate."

"And we just need two?" Dwight asked.

"Yup."

"That won't be hard."

"Not at all." We sat there, thinking. And thinking. And thinking.

"Maybe something on TV will give us an idea," Dwight said.

"No movies," I said. "We can't get distracted."

"Definitely no movies." Dwight flipped past the movie channels. "Hey, they're reshowing the video game awards."

"I missed them this year."

"Me, too." Dwight put the remote down.

It was an excellent show. So was the program after it that reviewed a bunch of new games.

"We have to go with one judge," I said on Thursday. "Meat, chocolate, or sports. We'll just have to hope one of the other judges likes our project, too."

"I vote for chocolate," Dwight said.

"Me, too. Everyone likes that. Let's see what we have around here." I went to the kitchen cabinet. "Score!" Mom had gone shopping the other day, and she'd bought a huge sack of chocolate bars.

I pulled them out. "We can make something. How about Joshua Stirling's cabin?"

"That would work," Dwight said. "But let me build it. You're not really good with your hands."

I didn't argue. Dwight might be an idiot, but he was great with tools and stuff. I could program all the electronics in the house and find stuff on the internet, but I pretty much stank at anything that required coordination. My drawings in art class looked like they were done during an earthquake, and I'm the only student in the history of our school who got banned from the woodshop.

"Okay," I said. "I'll go online and find a picture."

We got to work. I found a drawing that was pretty detailed, and Dwight did an amazing job with the construction. He cut out windows and stuff, and even made some smoke for the chimney with a cotton ball.

"This looks awesome," I said when he was finished. It was a perfect model of the cabin, made out of chocolate bars.

"I told you I do my best work the day before something is due." Dwight stepped back and stared at the cabin. "How do we explain why we made it out of chocolate?"

"We don't," I said. "Nobody is going to ask. Come on, let's put this somewhere safe."

Dwight and I picked up the cabin. He'd built it on a board we'd found in the basement. We carried it to the spare room. "It'll be safe here," I said as I closed the door.

"Think we'll win?" Dwight asked.

"We've got at least one vote," I said. "I'll see you in the morning. You can help me carry it to school."

I went back to the kitchen. The table was covered with leftover pieces of chocolate. There was no way I was going to throw any of that out, and I couldn't put it back in the bag, so I ate it all. That was a mistake. I gave myself a pretty bad stomachache.

Mom got all concerned when I didn't eat dinner and crawled up to bed early. But I told her I was fine. I was going to be even finer a week from now when I jumped into the wave pool at Splashtastic Park.

I woke up in the middle of the night, freezing. I really had to figure out a way to keep Dad from ever touching the thermostat. My stomach still hurt but not as badly. I staggered downstairs and switched on some heat, then hurried back upstairs because I had to go to the bathroom.

Friday morning, my first thought was *I'm sick*. I was burning hot. My pajamas were all soaked with sweat. But when I got out of bed, I felt fine. It was the room that was hot. I guess I'd set the temperature a bit too high. I'd been sort of in a rush last night.

There was a note from Mom taped to the bathroom mirror. "I hope you're feeling better. Call me at work if you're still sick and I'll come home."

Right after I got dressed, the doorbell rang. It was Dwight.

"You're kind of early," I said.

"I couldn't wait. This is going to be the best day ever." He grinned and held up a video camera.

"What's that for?"

"I want to get a shot of Zeke's face when he loses. Maybe I'll add music and put it on the internet. I have software that makes it all real easy."

"Perfect." I could just imagine Zeke's expression when the judges gave us first place.

I opened the door to the spare room and staggered back as a blast of warm air hit my face. Really warm air. *Oh no. . . .* The spare room was right above the furnace. I looked at the table. Joshua Stirling's cabin was now Lake Stirling.

"It melted," Dwight said.

"We lost," I said.

"No way. We can't let Zeke win."

I stared at the puddle of chocolate. We'd never be able to fix it.

"We gotta go with my first idea," Dwight said.

"We don't have time to make a cannon," I said.

"No. Not that. The mummy," he said. "Remember? It's perfect. We'll turn you into a mummy."

"Forget it. It's stupid. And it won't help us with any of the judges."

"No, it's not stupid. It's totally awesome. All the judges will love it," Dwight said. "Think about it. Everyone else will have boring stuff. We'll have a living, walking mummy."

"Yeah, and a living, walking loss to Zeke, or one of the other kids who had a week to do a project."

We argued about it for a while longer. Finally, I had to admit that it was our best idea. Mostly because it was our only idea. "But why me? Why don't we make you the mummy?" I asked.

"It was my idea," he said. "And I'm better with stuff like that than you are. If you wrapped me, I'd look like a Father's Day present from a five-year-old."

He was probably right. Besides, I guess it would be sort

of cool to stagger around school like a mummy.

"Come on," Dwight said. "Let's find some sheets."

I was glad that Mom had already left for work. I figured she'd have a problem with Dwight and me cutting up her sheets, but if I won a contest, she'd be so shocked I was betting she'd forgive me. I didn't exactly have a lot of victories in my past. That became real obvious last year when Mom decided to make one of those scrapbooks where you brag about all the stuff your family has done. After a couple days of finding nothing to scrap about, she gave up and decided it would be more fun to make flowerpots.

I went to the closet in the upstairs hallway where Mom kept the sheets, towels, and blankets.

"They're green," Dwight said as he leaned over my shoulder.

"Yeah. That's not gonna work." It looked like we were losers for sure.

"Mummies get old, right? So we could say it's moldy."

"That's completely stupid." I thought as hard as I could, and actually came up with a solution. "Hey—I know. We could paint them."

"Got any paint?"

"I'm not sure." I started looking through all the closets in the house. Finally, I found a shelf under the bathroom counter with first-aid stuff. "Bandages!" I shouted when I saw the boxes. My mom didn't just buy food at the warehouse store. We had big boxes of everything from garbage bags to detergent. So we had plenty of bandages. Each box had something ridiculous, like two hundred yards.

"We don't need sheets. We have real bandages." I dragged a box from the shelf and handed it to Dwight. "Wrap me up."

Dwight opened the box. He stared at the bandages for a moment, then stared at me. "I think you need to take off your shirt and pants."

"Why?"

"It'll look weird if you have clothes on under the bandages. Come on, take 'em off."

"I don't think so."

"You have to. We're going to be late."

"Okay. But I'm keeping my underwear." I pulled off my shirt and dropped my pants.

Dwight had trouble getting the first part of the bandage off the roll. But once he got started, he wrapped me real quickly. After he finished my right leg, he said, "This stuff is hard to tear. Got scissors?"

"No time for that. Just do it in one piece."

"Sure. There's plenty."

Dwight left slits for my eyes and nose. But he taped

over my mouth. He ended up using the whole box. Mom wouldn't miss it. There were several more boxes of bandages on the shelf.

Before we left, Dwight grabbed another box. "Just in case we need to patch you up or anything."

We headed out. I walked like a mummy, which was pretty easy since the bandages made it hard to bend any of my joints. I had to admit, I was starting to feel like we could actually win the contest.

Halfway down the block, Dwight handed me the extra box of bandages. "Here, hold this so I can get a good shot of you."

I took the box and Dwight held up the video camera. Then he took his right hand off of it and rubbed his thumb against his fingers. "Man, that stuff is really sticky."

"Sticky?" I glanced down at the box through the slits. According to the label, they were STAY-STUCK BRAND ADHE-SIVE BANDAGES.

Adhesive?

Below, a bit smaller, it read: WITH SUPER HOLDING POWER THAT NEVER LETS GO. And below that, even smaller: CAUTION: REMOVE SLOWLY.

I thought about what it felt like when I ripped even a small Band-Aid off my arm.

"You idiot!" I screamed at Dwight. It didn't come out as any real words, since my lips were taped over. I threw the box at him.

He ducked. "Hey! Watch out. You'll hit the camera."

I tugged at the end of the bandage, where it dangled from my hand. "It's all stuck to me!" I gave him a shove.

"Knock it off!" He shoved me back. "Dummy mummy."

I staggered and stepped off the curb, which made me stagger a couple more steps on my stiff legs. A car whizzed toward me. I looked right at the driver. He looked right at his cell phone.

I'm going to die.

I tried to spin out of the way. Luckily I didn't get hit. The car just nicked my finger as it shot past.

I'm going to live.

Before I could sigh in relief, I was yanked off my feet.

I'm flying?

The rear bumper had snagged the end of the bandage from the tip of my finger. I guess the driver was still on the phone, because he didn't seem to realize he was pulling me down the road. I managed to stay on my feet, but I felt like I was waterskiing. I yanked my hand back, hard.

That worked. The bandage started to unwind. My relief didn't last more than a second, though. After my arm got unwrapped, my body started to unwind. That made me spin. I was having a hard time staying on my feet. Everything was happening too fast. I was spinning, staggering, and skittering across the hard asphalt.

Oh yeah—and screaming. Especially when the unwinding reached my head and I felt my eyebrows get ripped off.

The bandage reached my left leg. I had to lift it in the air as it unwound, or my other leg would get tangled and I'd go down for sure. I was balancing on one foot now. I could smell burning rubber as my sneaker started to melt.

When the bandage reached my other leg, I realized I had an even bigger problem. The car made a right turn. The bandage pulled around the streetlight on the corner. I was getting yanked toward the pole. A lucky leap kept me from smacking right into it, but I was whipped around the corner and flung through the air. Now I really was flying. Finally, the end of the bandage was yanked from my leg, taking my sneaker with it.

I sailed across the street and thudded to a facedown landing. I was too dizzy to move. I hurt all over. And from the smell of it, I'd landed in the yard of someone who owned several enormous dogs. Which helped explain why I slid so far after I hit. But at least I'd survived. Dwight caught up with me, still carrying the camera.

"Oh no," he gasped.

"What?"

"Nothing." His voice sounded weird, and his face got as green as Mom's sheets.

"Tell me."

"I guess the adhesive kind of took a tiny little bit of skin with it."

And my shorts, I discovered as I glanced over my shoulder. They were gone. Ripped right off me. They'd saved my skin. At least, a little bit of skin where the shorts had been. As for the rest of me, above my waist and below my thighs, my body looked like I'd been peeled. It took a moment for that fact to sink into my numbed and dizzy brain. I stared at my hands and then down at my arms and legs.

I'd been peeled like an apple. No, more like a tomato. I looked like I had the worst case of sunburn the world had ever seen. The whole top layer of my skin was gone. It was a thin layer, but I had been kind of attached to it.

Then the pain kicked in. That's when I passed out.

I woke up in the hospital. It was Saturday. I was covered in real bandages this time. My parents were so happy I was alive that they didn't yell at me too much.

Dwight came to visit me that afternoon. "How you doing?" he asked.

"How does it look like I'm doing?"

"It looks really cool. Too bad it's nowhere near Halloween."

I sighed. "I guess Zeke won."

"No way. Check this out." He held up the video camera and started playing a clip.

I saw a title on the screen.

NEW CAIRO

From Mummies to Medicine

150 Years in 150 Seconds

Then I saw myself walking along in my original mummy outfit. I winced as I watched my unwinding body spin and tumble like a really bad gymnast's. I cringed as the camera zoomed in on my peeled body. In the middle of all that red flesh, my white butt looked like a blob of mayonnaise on a boiled hot dog.

My own screams were replaced by those of sirens. The paramedics showed up. Dwight had recorded the whole trip to the emergency room and all the action of the doctors and nurses working on my damaged body. Then he'd edited everything down to the highlights.

"You showed this at school?" I couldn't believe all the kids had seen me sprawled out on the ground, barer than naked. I'd have to move to another town. No, another planet. Even that might not be far enough. "Everyone saw it?"

"Yeah. Sure. Nobody else did a video, so they let me play it on the big screen in the auditorium."

"And the judges liked it?"

"Well, the chocolate lady and the sports guy both threw up and ran out of the room right after you got peeled. But the butcher loved the whole thing. So, like you said, you appealed to one judge." Dwight paused, frowned, then said, "Wait . . . peeled . . . appealed. I think there's some kind of connection."

"Drop it," I said. "What happened after that?"

"Since the butcher was the only one left to vote, we won first prize. I'm going to Splashtastic Park. And here's your half of the bet." He put a twenty-dollar bill on my chest.

As I looked down at the money, I thought about his words. *I'm going to Splashtastic Park.* "You mean *we're* going to Splashtastic Park."

"You really want to wade into salt water next week?" Dwight asked.

I imagined how that would feel on my peeled body. It would definitely sting. "I guess not."

"That's what I thought. So I asked Zeke."

"Zeke!" I bolted up. That was a huge mistake. I felt like someone had just swiped my whole body with an enormous piece of sandpaper.

I let out a scream and slumped back down.

"Yeah, Zeke," Dwight said. "I've been thinking about things, and even if you got out of here in time, I'm pretty sure it's a better idea if I go to Splashtastic Park with someone smarter. You'd probably get us kicked out five minutes after we got there. No offense. You're a good friend and all. You're loyal. You're courageous. But you have to admit, you're sort of an idiot."

I opened my mouth to argue. *No, Dwight, you're the idiot.* Then I closed my mouth. What could I say? Dwight was right. He was going to Splashtastic Park. He was a winner. He had all his skin. I was the kid who let someone cover him in bandages and walk him down the street. I was an idiot. A skinless, bandaged idiot.

"Well, I'd like to hang around," Dwight said, "but Zeke won a couple movie tickets for second place, and he's sharing them with me. The show's starting soon. I gotta go." He headed out.

I stayed where I was. Skinless. Friendless. Prizeless.

Well, it could be worse. At least I'd have a lot of scabs to pick soon. I wondered whether I could grind them up and sell them for medicine. Then I could start my own town. I guess I could call it Stupidville.

YOUR QUESTION FOR AUTHOR HERE

BY KATE DiCAMILLO & JON SCIESZKA

DEAR MRS. O'TOOPLE,

WE ARE READING THIS BOOK IN SCHOOL WHERE A KID WRITES TO AN AUTHOR.

SO WE HAVE TO WRITE TO AN AUTHOR.

WE ARE ALSO STUDYING "PARTS OF A FRIENDLY LETTER."

SO THIS IS ALSO A FRIENDLY LETTER.

IN THE BOOK WE ARE READING THIS KID THINKS THE AUTHOR'S BOOKS ARE REALLY GREAT AND THEN THE AUTHOR WRITES BACK AND SAVES THE KID'S LIFE OR SOMETHING. I'M NOT SURE BECAUSE I ONLY READ THE FIRST PART OF THE BOOK.

PLEASE SEND A BUNCH OF AUTHOR STUFF SO WE CAN GET THIS OVER WITH.

CLOSING,

JOE JONES

Dear Joe Jones,

You have reached Maureen O'Toople. I am quite sure, however, that you have not reached her using the method your teacher suggested. Your teacher asked you to pen a Friendly Letter. The letter I received from you was not Friendly. It was, rather, Perfunctory.

And look, I have written you a Perfunctory Letter in return. There's a certain symmetry to that, isn't there?

Yours in the spirit of getting this over with,
Maureen O'Toople

P. S. I'm afraid I have no idea what "author stuff" is. Therefore, I will be unable to send you any.

DEAR MAUREEN O'TOOPLE,

WHAT THE HECK KIND OF AUTHOR LETTER WAS THAT? I AM SUPPOSED TO ASK THE QUESTIONS. YOU ARE SUPPOSED TO SEND BACK THE AUTHOR ANSWERS. THAT'S HOW THE ASSIGNMENT GOES. THAT IS ALL YOU HAVE TO DO.

THERE'S NOTHING IN THE ASSIGNMENT ABOUT WRITING A PERFUNCTORY LETTER. BUT MAYBE I CAN GET SOME EXTRA CREDIT BECAUSE I DID THAT, TOO.

SO HERE ARE THE QUESTIONS, RIGHT OFF THE BOARD, JUST HOW MRS. BUND WROTE THEM.

1. WHY DO YOU WRITE BOOKS?
2. WHERE DO YOU GET YOUR IDEAS?
3. WHAT GOT YOU STARTED WRITING?
4. YOUR QUESTION FOR AUTHOR HERE.

PLEASE SEND SOME GOOD AUTHOR ANSWERS OR MRS. BUND WILL GIVE ME ANOTHER C- AND THEN MY MOM WILL FREAK OUT AGAIN AND SAY I'M NOT APPLYING MYSELF AND MY DAD WILL GROUND ME AND I WILL MISS MY BASEBALL TEAM PLAYOFFS AND HAVE TO DO WHATEVER THEY SAY FOR THE NEXT WEEK.

I'M NOT KIDDING,

JOE JONES

Dear Joe Jones,

No one gets credit for writing Perfunctory Letters. They are an insult to the human spirit. What we humans crave is connection. Perfunctory Letters work counter to that.

But I digress; I digress!

You have posed some questions. And you want some answers, answers that will result in you receiving a grade higher than a C—. I don't know if I can help you, Joe, because I don't feel like answering questions. The older you get, the more questions you get asked, and the more weary you become of answering the questions and the more elusive the answers—any answer, every answer—seem.

What I _would_ like to do is ask a question. I would like to ask you a question. So, let's make a deal, Joe. I'll ask you a question and you answer it. And then, if I feel like it, I'll answer one of your questions. How does that sound?

Here's my first question for you: Are you afraid of thunderstorms?

Yours cordially and only somewhat perfunctorily
and more than a little curiously,
Maureen O'Toople

P. S. I'm no fool, Joe. I'm betting good money
that you haven't read one single book I've written.
Prove me wrong.

MAUREEN O'TOOPLE,

AW, COME ON. IT'S BAD ENOUGH I HAVE TO DO THIS LAME ASSIGNMENT. NOW I HAVE TO WRITE EXTRA? I THOUGHT AUTHORS WERE SUPPOSED TO LIKE GETTING LETTERS FROM THEIR KID FANS.

BUT IF I DON'T GET THESE ANSWERS, I AM HOSED. THAT'S WHAT MY DAD SAYS. HOSED. I DON'T KNOW WHAT THAT REALLY MEANS. LIKE, WHAT DOES A HOSE HAVE TO DO WITH ANYTHING? BUT I DO KNOW IT MEANS NO TV, NO COMPUTER TIME, NO BASEBALL, NO COMICS, NO MUSIC, NO PHONE, NO HANGING OUT WITH MY FRIEND JAMES. BASICALLY IT MEANS NOTHING THAT IS REALLY THE GOOD PART OF LIVING.

WHY WOULD THEY DO THAT TO ME? DO PEOPLE JUST GET MEANER WHEN THEY GET OLDER?

OKAY, HERE'S MY ANSWER. I AM KIND OF AFRAID OF THUNDERSTORMS. NOT THE RAIN PART. THAT SOUNDS GREAT ON THE ROOF. IT'S THE PART BETWEEN THE FLASH OF LIGHTNING AND THE BAM OF THUNDER. IT'S WAITING FOR THE BAM THAT WEIRDS ME OUT. YOU JUST DON'T KNOW WHEN IT'S GOING TO HAPPEN.

SO PLEASE SEND ME SOME AUTHOR ANSWERS. AS SOON AS YOU CAN.

REALLY,

JOE JONES

P. S. I DIDN'T GET A CHANCE TO READ ANY OF YOUR BOOKS YET. I ACTUALLY PICKED YOU MOSTLY TO ANNOY JENNIFER, BECAUSE SHE IS ALL CRAZY ABOUT YOUR BOOKS AND ALWAYS TALKING ABOUT THE HORSES OR THE PRINCESSES OR WHATEVER IS IN THEM. I USUALLY ONLY READ HISTORY BOOKS THAT REALLY TELL YOU SOMETHING. AND BOOKS THAT ARE FUNNY.

Dear Joe,

Thank you for answering my question. I, too, like the sound of the rain on the roof. I also like the lightning. It's like some great cosmic flashlight. It makes me think that someone is searching for me. And I don't mind the BAM of thunder because that makes me think that, perhaps, I have been found. That's the way a good book makes me feel, as if I have been found, understood, seen.

Oh, I'm sneaky, Joe. Right there, in the first paragraph, I have answered your first question. And you know what that means: Now I get to ask you another question. Are you ready?

What's in your sock drawer besides socks?

That's the question. Answer it and I'll answer another question of yours. Quid pro quo.

Amusing myself
and delighted to be a part of your "lame assignment"
I remain,
Maureen

P. S. "Whatever is in them" is a truly alarming phrase to use in reference to my books. But, as an interesting aside, I am happy to inform you that none of my books (not one) features princesses or horses. Toads, tidal waves, arachnid revolutions, yes. Princesses, no. Horses, no. Do your research, Joe.

P. P. S. Yes. People do get meaner as they get older.

MAUREEN,

HA! YOU ARE COMPLETELY NOT GOING TO BELIEVE WHAT I HAVE IN MY SOCK DRAWER BESIDES SOCKS: SPIDERS. OR ARACHNIDS, AS THEY ARE SCIENTIFICALLY CALLED. ONE IS A WOLF SPIDER. THE THREE OTHER ONES ARE JUMPING SPIDERS. I HAVE TO HIDE THEM IN MY SOCK DRAWER SO MY MOM DOESN'T MAKE ME THROW THEM OUT.

IT'S ALSO A GOOD WAY TO KEEP MY SISTER OUT OF MY SOCK DRAWER. BECAUSE I ALSO HAVE ROCKS I HAVE COLLECTED FROM ALL OVER THE COUNTRY, A REAL ARROWHEAD I FOUND LAST SUMMER, AND A REAL CIVIL WAR BULLET. IT'S CALLED A MINIÉ BALL. AND NOT BECAUSE IT IS MINI. OR A BALL. IT WAS NAMED AFTER THIS GUY MINIÉ WHO INVENTED THE RIFLE USED A LOT IN THE CIVIL WAR. IT IS MADE OF LEAD.

BUT YOU ARE STILL REALLY MESSING UP THIS ASSIGNMENT. HOW IS THAT AN ANSWER TO QUESTION ONE? ARE YOU SAYING YOU WRITE BOOKS BECAUSE YOU LIKE LIGHTNING AND DON'T MIND THUNDER? THAT'S WHAT I'M WRITING DOWN.

JOE

P. S. SORRY I WAS ALARMING YOU TALKING ABOUT YOUR BOOKS. I WENT AND LOOKED AT THE SPIDER ONE IN THE LIBRARY. THE FIRST PART OF FANGS FOR THE DUCHESS IS PRETTY GOOD. MOST PEOPLE DON'T KNOW THAT SPIDERS SQUIRT VENOM INTO THEIR PREY THAT DISSOLVES THEIR INNARDS SO THEY CAN SUCK IT DOWN. I'M GLAD YOU HAD THAT IN THERE.

BUT THE TITLE IS STILL PRETTY PRINCESS-Y.

Dear Joe,

Arachnids in your sock drawer! I'm impressed. Truly. But I must take issue with the notion that I am messing up this assignment. What I am doing is enriching your life. And sometimes, in dark and confusing moments, I think that you might be enriching mine. For instance, I have read quite a bit about the Civil War, but I did not know about this gentleman Minié and his invention of the minié ball. Many young boys, boys almost as young as you, went off to fight in the Civil War. I bet you know that. But just think: That minié ball you have could have hit one of those boys on the battlefield, grazed his check, wounded him, left him scarred. Who was that boy? What was his name? What story would he tell about that piece of lead in your sock drawer?

Oh, I delight myself. Why? Because I just answered question number two, that's why. As for the thunder and the lightning, the BAM and the flashlight, it's like this, Joe: If a good book can make you feel found, seen, wouldn't you want to try and work the magic of finding, seeing another? Huh? Wouldn't you?

Yours,
Maureen

P. S. I have a truly world-class arrowhead collection.

DEAR MAUREEN,

THAT IS PRETTY CRAZY THAT SOMEBODY LIKE ME AND
JAMES WOULD BE SNEAKING AROUND THE WOODS IN VIRGINIA OR
PENNSYLVANIA TRYING TO SHOOT OTHER KIDS JUST LIKE US. IT WOULD
BE KIND OF LIKE BATTLING IN A BASEBALL SERIES, BUT WITH GUNS.
THAT COULD REALLY CHANGE THE WHOLE STORY OF SOMEONE'S LIFE.

OH, I ALSO FORGOT TO TELL YOU ANOTHER THING I HAVE IN MY
SOCK DRAWER. A HALF-FINISHED BAG OF CHEETOS. JUST IN CASE YOU
NEED THAT FOR YOUR AUTHOR ANSWERS.

AND I THINK I UNDERSTAND YOUR CRAZY ANSWERS, BUT COULD
YOU SPEED IT UP? SINCE I DON'T HAVE ALL MY ANSWERS, I CAN'T PUT
YOUR LETTER UP ON MRS. BUND'S AUTHOR LETTER BOARD. AND THEN
I GOT IN TROUBLE WITH OUR GYM TEACHER, MR. BROWN, BECAUSE
I WAS LATE FOR CLASS BECAUSE I WAS EXPLAINING THINGS TO
MRS. BUND. AND THEN I GOT IN TROUBLE WITH THE PRINCIPAL, MR.
BARNETT, BECAUSE MR. BROWN THOUGHT I WAS TALKING BACK TO
HIM. AND PARENT/TEACHER NIGHT IS COMING UP AND I AM GOING TO
REALLY GET IT. SO THIS IS KIND OF ALL YOUR FAULT.

AND NOW ON TOP OF ALL OF THAT, WE HAVE TO WRITE A POEM.
HOLY CRAP. I KNOW I'M NOT SUPPOSED TO BE CURSING TO AN AUTHOR.
BUT COULD YOU JUST WRITE ME A POEM? IT WOULD REALLY HELP ME
OUT. YOU COULD WRITE IT ABOUT YOUR ARROWHEADS. WHAT KINDS DO
YOU HAVE?

YOURS,

JOE

Dear Joe,

As friendly as I am feeling toward you right now (I was impressed with your powers of empathy and imagination vis-à-vis the boys of the Civil War), I will not write you a poem. I, Maureen O'Toople, will NEVER AGAIN be involved in any nefarious activity. Don't ask me to define "nefarious." Suffice it to say that I have done wrong and that my bad behavior resulted in a small amount of time in the hoosegow. Yes, Joe, jail. I, Maureen O'Toople, have been in jail. And it was there, in the dark confines of my cell, that I decided to change my life, to work as much good in the world as I was capable of working.

But I digress. Fortunately, my digression answered another of your questions! Yes, there it is: The answer to question number three. That means that you are that much closer to getting to post my letter on the bulletin board (what a happy day that will be). It also means that I get to ask you another question. Here it is.

What phase is the moon in?

Your writer friend,

Maureen

P. S. I know that you are worried about your poem assignment. I can sense your anxiety from here. I am going to take pity on you. I will show you how simple it is to write a poem. Look around you. Look inside you. Like this, Joe:

WHY I WRITE
I like lightning and
thunder, flashlight and the BAM:
looking, being found.

Don't panic. You can do it, too. The first line of a haiku is five syllables. The second is seven syllables. And the third line is five syllables. Those are the guidelines. But within the confines of those rules, the sky is the limit. Anything and everything belongs in a poem.

P. P. S. Please don't steal my poem and turn it in as yours, Joe.

MAUREEN,

YOU ARE KIND OF DRIVING ME CRAZY. MOST ADULTS JUST BOSS KIDS AROUND AND MAKE THEM DO STUFF JUST BECAUSE THEY SAY SO. BUT YOU ARE MORE LIKE THE LIGHTNING, AND THEN I'M THINKING ABOUT IT AND BAM, THERE'S THE THUNDER. ARE YOU A CRAZY, PSYCHIC OCEANOGRAPHER LIKE THE ONE IN YOUR BOOK <u>MOTHER TIDE</u>? I LIKED THE PART ABOUT ALL OF THE CITIES BEING WIPED OUT BY THE GIANT WAVES. BUT WHY DID YOU WAIT SO LONG TO GET TO THAT GOOD PART OF THE STORY? ALSO THERE SEEMED TO BE TOO MUCH TALKING BEFORE THE WAVES.

ANYWAY, I USED YOUR IDEA OF ANYTHING AND EVERYTHING FOR A POEM. THIS IS IT.

<u>WHAT I HAVE</u>
CIVIL WAR BULLET
THE STORY OF SOMEONE'S LIFE
HIDES IN MY SOCK DRAWER.

I GAVE IT TO MRS. BUND AND SHE WAS PRETTY SURPRISED. SHE EVEN LOOKED LIKE SHE WAS STARTING TO CRY A LITTLE. THEN SHE ASKED ME IF I COPIED IT FROM SOMEPLACE ELSE. I TOLD HER NO BUT I GOT SOME HELP FROM THE AUTHOR ASSIGNMENT I WAS STILL WORKING ON. I GOT A B. SO I GUESS YOU DO KNOW WHAT YOU ARE DOING WITH AUTHOR STUFF.

OH, AND I ALMOST FORGOT—YOU WENT TO JAIL? I'LL BET YOU WERE A SPY OR MAYBE A NINJA CAT BURGLAR. I DON'T THINK

YOU WERE ROBBING BANKS OR MUGGING OLD LADIES. I HOPE YOU WEREN'T. WERE YOU?

I THINK THIS IS THE LONGEST LETTER I HAVE EVER WRITTEN. AND I STILL HAVE TO ANSWER YOUR QUESTION AND GIVE YOU MY LAST QUESTION. OKAY. THE MOON IS WAXING GIBBOUS. THAT MEANS IT IS GETTING MORE FULL. AND I HAVE NO IDEA WHY YOU NEED TO KNOW THAT.

SO THE LAST QUESTION FOR THE AUTHOR ASSIGNMENT. I WAS JUST MESSING AROUND WITH YOU BEFORE WHEN I WROTE THAT #4, "YOUR QUESTION HERE."

MY LAST AUTHOR QUESTION REALLY IS—HOW DO YOU KNOW IF YOU MIGHT BE A WRITER?

YOUR KID-IN-SCHOOL PAL,

JOE

Dear Joe,

First, allow me to say how delighted I am that you read (and offered an honest—if somewhat flawed—critique) of <u>Mother Tide</u>. It makes me happy that you are going to the library and looking for the books that bear my name. Look for other books, too.

And more happy news: You wrote your own poem! And it's a good one. You took your sock drawer and its contents and applied your imagination and your heart to them and made a wonderful poem. I'm so happy that you got a B. Personally, I would have given you an A. But then, what do I know? I'm just a writer who was once incarcerated.

And speaking of my incarceration, I was not a ninja cat burglar. Or a spy. I am somebody who made a mistake. And when I had the time to consider (there in my filthy jail cell) what I had done and who I was, I decided that I could and would rewrite the story of my life. And I have. Every book I write helps me to understand myself better and to love the world more.

Which brings me to your last question. And that question is: How do you know if you are a writer? For once, I am going to answer a question as directly as I am able. My answer goes like this: You know that you are a writer if you are imaginative. You know that you are a writer if you are curious. You know that you are a writer if you are interested in the things and people of the world. You know that you are a writer if you hold a minié ball in your hand and wonder about its story. You know that you are a writer if you like the sound of rain on the roof. And if you want to tell someone else about your heart and how waiting for the thunder sometimes makes you feel, if you work to find the words to do that, then you are a writer.

So, guess what, Joe?

You're a writer.

I remain,

your fellow writer,

Maureen

P. S. Yes, the moon is a waxing gibbous. Isn't it wonderful to look up at the sky and to know what the moon is doing, to have a name for it and to know that other people, people far away, are looking up at the same moon and saying the same words, "waxing gibbous, waxing gibbous," along with you?

P. P. S. I wonder if you will write another haiku? There's something sad and wonderful about a half-eaten bag of Cheetos.

Maureen,

I turned in my answers for the Write an Author Project. I got a C-. I put in the part about the way a good book makes you feel found. I put in the minié ball and asking questions. I put in you going to the hoosegow. I really wrote this. And I got a C-.

So now everything is messed up. My mom and dad say I just don't care. No TV, computer, phone, friends, or fun. I'm grounded for the next four years at least. So that means I miss the championship game next weekend against CWI Woodworking. And everybody is going to hate me for not showing up.

The gym teacher, Mr. Brown, hates me. Principal Barnett yells at me. The librarian, Mrs. Morris, won't let me pick out my own books anymore. Even the lunch ladies are wrecking my chicken fingers now.

Mrs. Bund didn't even put any of your letters up on the Author Letter Board.

That's all,

Joe Jones

P. S. I was going to read your Luna-Tales book, but now I'm going to take it back to the library.

Dear Joe,

This letter of yours is almost more than I can bear. It is, in fact, <u>more</u> than I can bear. I will not stand idly by. No, I will not. I am taking action, Joe.

Please have your parents bring you to the airport on Monday at 2:20 p.m. I will be arriving to your fair city on Nifty Airlines, Flight 2012. I will wait for you in baggage claim. You will know me by the purple scarf wound around my neck. You will know me as one writer knows another.

It's time to turn this story around.

Adieu until Monday,

Maureen

P. S. We didn't even make it up on the bulletin board?

MAUREEN,

I CAN'T BELIEVE IT. THE WHOLE SCHOOL IS STILL CRAZY AFTER YOUR VISIT. MR. BROWN HAS US RUNNING YOUR NFL DRILLS. MRS. MORRIS SMILES AT ME, AND NOW SHE REMEMBERS MY NAME. MR. BARNETT CALLS ME CHAMP EVERY TIME HE SEES ME AND ASKS HOW YOU ARE DOING. THE LUNCH LADIES ARE EVEN COOKING THE CHICKEN FINGERS THE WAY YOU SHOWED THEM! AND THEY ARE WAY BETTER. THE CHICKEN FINGERS. NOT THE LUNCH LADIES.

I'M ALSO PRETTY FAMOUS WITH THE GIRLS NOW THAT THEY KNOW YOU AND ME WRITE STUFF TOGETHER. I'LL TRY TO READ SOME MORE OF YOUR BOOKS, BUT I HAVE TO SAY I STILL THINK THEY ARE A LITTLE BIT GIRL-ISH. NOT TOTALLY. YOU DO HAVE A LOT OF STUFF THAT REALLY GRABS A READER LIKE A MONGOOSE GRABS A COBRA BY THE THROAT AND THRASHES IT AROUND UNTIL IT IS BLOODY AND DEAD (OUR LATEST ENGLISH ASSIGNMENT IS WRITING METAPHORS AND SIMILES).

MRS. BUND DOESN'T LIKE TO TALK ABOUT YOUR VISIT TOO MUCH AFTER WHAT HAPPENED IN THE READ AND SHARE PART OF CLASS. BUT SHE DID SAY IT CHANGED HER LIFE. YESTERDAY SHE TOOK DOWN THE AUTHOR BOARD AND SAID WE DON'T NEED TO WRITE TO AUTHORS EVER AGAIN.

AND IT'S NOT PART OF AN ASSIGNMENT OR ANYTHING, BUT I MADE UP ANOTHER HAIKU.

WHAT AUTHOR KICKS BUTT
AND MAKES PEOPLE GLAD SHE DID?
MAUREEN O'TOOPLE.

OH, AND THANKS THE MOST FOR YOUR TIP ABOUT MY BATTING STANCE.
I WENT 3 FOR 5 WITH 4 RBIs. WE KILLED CWI WOODWORKING, 8–3.
WE ARE THE CHAMPS.

MY MOM SAYS TO GIVE YOU A HUG AND A KISS. MY DAD SAYS YOU
ARE A REAL CHARACTER. I THINK YOU TURNED OUT TO BE A PRETTY
GOOD AUTHOR TO PICK EVEN IF I DID DO IT TO BUG JENNIFER.

GOOD LUCK WITH YOUR WRITING STUFF. I THINK I MIGHT WORK
SOME MORE ON MY STORY "CIVIL WAR SOLDIERS UNDER THE WAXING
GIBBOUS MOON." LET ME KNOW IF YOU NEED ANY HELP WITH YOUR
STORIES. I'VE GOT PLENTY MORE IDEAS.

YOUR WRITING PAL,

JOE JONES

Dear Champ,

I can't wait to read "Civil War Soldiers under the Waxing Gibbous Moon." It sounds like it will be a fantastic book. Maybe after you are done writing it and I am done reading it, I will write you a letter and you will answer it and we will become friends.

Wouldn't that make a great story?

Thank you, Joe.

Maureen

P. S. That last haiku of yours was one of the best poems I have ever read.

A FISTFUL OF FEATHERS
BY DAVID YOO

One night in the fall of fifth grade my dad finally got fed up with me and decided it was time to make me a man. Translation: My dad thought I was positively girly and was worried that I'd get bullied once I got to middle school the next year. He had been appalled earlier that day to see that only girls had been invited to my eleventh birthday party, and that night he glared at me all through dinner as I nibbled on a tofu burger (I'd been a vegetarian since the third grade, when I bit into an unbelievably purply, bloody Chicken McNugget at McDonald's), before finally announcing, "That's it, I'm making you my special project, Sam. We're going to right this ship starting tomorrow."

Had I been born in previous generations, my dad telling

me he was going to make a man out of me would have meant taking me hunting for the first time, or letting me take a sip of his beer as we watched baseball on TV, or spending the fall making a soapbox racer together, but he had other ideas for how to make me less girly.

Before I continue, let me make it clear that it wasn't so much that I was girly as it was that my dad was the manliest boy growing up, ever. His own father was a lifelong military man, and my dad was born macho. He was that kid who never said no to a dare, rode a mini motorcycle at age eight (without a helmet, even), was the star linebacker of his Pop Warner football team. He shot BB guns and got into fights, and he was obsessed with fires—if he wasn't setting them for fun, he was pretending there was one and pulling the fire alarm at school.

I'll be the first to admit I wasn't a spitting image of my dad, not by a long shot. I didn't like to kill things with BB guns. I wasn't into pulling fire alarms and aimlessly riding bikes all over the neighborhood all day, and I didn't get a thrill from jumping off really high things for no good reason. Even if something was on fire or sinking or about to explode, you'd probably still have had a hard time getting me to jump. So sue me.

But for my dad, it was more than that. Or rather, it was

everything about me that seemed wrong. Truth be told, I didn't have any guy friends, but that wasn't really my fault; we lived on a street that had three girls in my grade and no boys, so I had no choice but to hang out with the ladies. But what really bugged him was that even my imaginary friend was a girl. Her name was Elizabeth, and I'd invented her back in third grade so I could have someone to play dolls with when the twins weren't around (I'll explain that in a moment), and we'd been best pals ever since. Even though she wasn't even real, my dad was still disgusted.

"Even your imaginary friend's a girl?" he'd groan anytime he caught me having a really loud conversation with nobody else in the room.

To make him feel better, I changed her name to Mr. Elizabeth, but it didn't help matters. I explained that he should've felt grateful that I'd changed her name at all but that I couldn't change her actual name—I mean, that would only confuse her, right? "Besides," I added, "what difference does it make what her name is if she's invisible. Shouldn't calling her Mr. Elizabeth be enough to make you happy?"

"I don't even know where to begin explaining just how messed up that is," he said, and left the room.

I kept the name Mr. Elizabeth anyway, because she

was a tomboy and it turned out she actually really liked the name. I considered telling my dad the good news but wisely figured he'd only hate me more.

Instead of doing typical "boy" things, I was creative as a kid, and of course my dad considered any type of creativity a girly quality. For example, he hated that I liked to draw. It's not like I drew unicorns and flowers with smiley faces and rainbows all day, but that I didn't at least draw realistic pictures of gun battles and spaceships bothered him. Instead, I preferred to draw nature scenes featuring really realistic cats, because I'd always wanted one, and I guess he considered a cat similar enough to a unicorn and this made him feel positively icky.

But did that make me any less of a man than all the other boys in my grade? I didn't think so. Okay, so maybe I liked to weave friendship bracelets in my spare time—which I'd learned how to make at summer camp (that my dad forced me to attend in the first place). And I admit I played with Polly Pocket dolls, which are intended for girls, at least according to the packaging (personally, I felt they were for anyone with a wonderful imagination). But again, this had more to do with my surroundings than me as a person: I played with Polly Pockets because my parents didn't buy me action figures (they were paranoid that my infant sister would try to eat them), and so I had to make do with the Benson twins' toy collection next door. If my dad caught me playing with the dolls, I'd immediately switch from trying out different outfits on them (for a tea party) and instead pretend that they were having a battle royale to the death. After he'd leave the room, I'd quietly apologize to the dolls and make sure they were okay.

"Sorry, ladies," I'd whisper. "Now who wants ice cream?"

My mom would always try to make me feel better whenever she witnessed my dad being appalled at my playing with dolls and stuff, and she'd always say the same thing: "Your father always wanted a boy." I knew what she meant—what she was trying to do was remind me that my dad, despite the way he grimaced all the time around me, really did always want a son and that I should feel welcome around him, which of course had the opposite effect. I mean, when a parent feels compelled to tell their child that their father really did want to have him, you know that's not a good sign.

Mom was probably the worst consoler in the history of mankind. She tried way too hard to make me feel better by saying things like that, which would always end up making me feel ten times worse. Like after I struggled with my first-ever swimming lesson, swallowing a mouthful of chlorine as the instructor had us hold the side of the pool and practice holding our breath underwater, Mom patted me on the head on the ride home and said, "Not everyone was meant to swim." Up to that moment I'd been planning on sticking it out for at least a second day but immediately decided I wasn't ever going to be able to do it. Or there was that time we spent a week at a beach house on the Cape, and one rainy afternoon I lost to her in a game of Concentration and she said, "Don't feel bad. We did drop you on your head once when you were really little."

And now she was telling me that Dad had always wanted a boy, thinking I felt unloved, which I did. I was failing in my dad's eyes, yet again. And she was wrong, for that matter—my dad didn't want just any old boy; specifically, he wanted a boy that was just like he was when he grew up. Which I clearly wasn't.

Hence the problem.

And so that's why that night at dinner my dad said he was going to make a man out of me. It was a vague statement, but somehow I knew to fear it.

"Thanksgiving's coming," he said, changing the subject, clicking his teeth as he pretended to hold up a drumstick. I played with the oversteamed, mushy carrots on my plate.

"Gross," I muttered, picturing him eating turkey.

He frowned.

"I don't know what his problem is," he said as if I couldn't hear him. "Everyone loves Thanksgiving. Must be the neighborhood. When I was seven, I played touch football with the older kids and ate red meat five times a week."

He looked at me, and I looked away.

"He plays with girls. You've been to our farm, Grace. We raised our own darn turkeys every fall. And we didn't have much money. Made you appreciate what a good Thanksgiving dinner's all about. Maybe that's what he needs."

Mom sighed.

"Only two weeks till Thanksgiving," she said.

They looked at each other. She shook her head, not looking at me.

"I just think it's so unnatural. It's not a healthy way to grow up," Dad went on. "Kids need to have tradition."

"Oh, please, Martin," she replied. "He's just more creatively inclined."

My dad just kept staring at me as if I was a stranger, and it made me feel really uncomfortable, but I now know that all the while he was coming up with the plan in his head to make me less girly, and in the end I have to admit the plan worked, although not nearly in the way anyone could have ever guessed.

* * *

The next morning from the window I watched Tracy, the babysitter, pull up in the rain. Mom handed the baby over to Tracy under the front stoop. Mom looked like she was giving directions, gesturing with her hands. A minute later my parents left in the SUV. Tracy came inside, and I followed her into the baby's room and watched her change the baby's diaper.

"Want to help me re-dye my hair?" she asked.

"Duh. Of course," I replied. "I'll go get the tinfoil from the kitchen."

An hour later I was watching TV downstairs when my parents got home. Mom took my hand and made me visit the baby again. We listened over the light snoring and the hum of the humidifier to the sounds in the backyard. I started to head over to the window to see what the noise was, but Mom pulled me back. She smiled at me.

"We have a surprise for you, Tiger."

I stared at the window, my mind racing.

"Okay, everything's set," Dad said as he bounded into the room two hours later. Mom had fallen asleep on the floor, and I was in the process of starving to death. "C'mere, Sammy."

He scooped me up; I tried to smile but his hands were

digging into my armpits. He settled me on his shoulders and carried me down the stairs. When we got outside, Dad put me on the ground, and I stared at the pen by the basement doors. The chicken fence. The dark shadow inside. I edged backward. Dad pushed me forward.

"Go see," he whispered.

We crowded around the pen. In a whoosh of feathers, the turkey emerged from the darkness. It was large with brown feathers and scaly claws. It hobbled around the small fenced-in space outside the pen.

"He's so adorable," Mom said, holding the baby, pointing at the pen, kissing the baby, pointing again.

"This one was the biggest of them all," Dad said. "We barely have to feed it. I think this will be good for Sam. Kids like animals; this is just the thing."

"But what if he gets attached to it?"

"You're missing the point, Grace. It's the tradition of raising a turkey. It teaches things. Having this bird around will get him into the spirit of Thanksgiving. That's what it's all about. It's simple math. Sam keeps eating tofu and he stays the smallest kid in his class, and that's just going to make life harder the older he gets."

She nodded.

"This is going to make him a man," he continued. "I

can't make him good at sports, and maybe I can't make him get real friends, but this . . . this has to work!"

Dad took the turkey out and set it on the ground.

"Will it try to run away?" I asked.

"No," he replied. "Birds are pretty stupid, especially turkeys; they're like glorified chickens. Don't be afraid."

I inched closer to the turkey and held out a hand. Suddenly the turkey lashed out, clamping its beak on my hand. It didn't hurt, but the sudden movement startled me and I said something I shouldn't have.

"Don't use the Lord's name in vain!" Dad shouted.

"He's barely spoken this whole afternoon, and when he does, this!" Mom said, pointing at the space in front of my mouth as if she could see the dirty words.

I was visibly shaken, and attached myself to the dogwood tree next to the garden. Dad stormed up the steps of the back porch and let the screen door slam behind him. The turkey did a circle on the grass. It pecked at the ground.

"Listen, Sam," Mom whispered soothingly. "Your daddy just wants you to appreciate Thanksgiving. This turkey means a lot to him. He spent all afternoon setting up the pen. Will you please come over here and just try, for Mommy, to get to know the turkey?"

I shuffled my feet in the thick green grass. The turkey

hopped back two steps. It stared at me with red eyes, and I gasped.

"See, it likes you." She laughed. The baby burped. Dad was watching from an open window above us.

"Give it a name," he called down to me.

"Um . . . Turkey?" I suggested.

Dad rolled his eyes at Mom.

"Yeah, he's the creative one all right," he said. Then he stared down into the turkey's devil red eyes for a couple of seconds. "I'm thinking your name is . . . Travis."

"Travis the turkey?" I asked.

Dad glared at me.

"It's a wonderful name, Martin," Mom added.

I watched as she placed the turkey back in the pen. The sun was going down, past the trees in the backyard, and the wind felt cold. We went inside.

That night, I sat next to the window in my bedroom on the second floor with the lights off, staring down at the pen. The sound of the baby's humidifier in the next room, through the thin walls. The house creaking as it braced against the wind. Downstairs, I could hear the faint sounds of clapping and laughter from the TV, followed by deep laughter from my dad.

The roof of the pen was a wide sheet of strip metal. Occasionally it clanged as a breeze swept across the backyard. The roof seemed to shimmer in the moonlight. I could make out a dozen half-bent nails sticking out of the wood on the side. The turkey was moving, bumping into the chicken wire with its beak. Inside the pen it was dark. I couldn't even make out a shadow. The light in the kitchen flicked on, and suddenly I saw the turkey. It was staring up at me, motionless, its red eyes gleaming in the light from the kitchen window. I was at first frozen, then dove out of view, two hops to the bed.

I slept with the blanket over my head.

"Will you look at this," Dad exclaimed, shaking his head at the window.

It was the next afternoon, and we were all sitting in the den, watching TV. The baby was upstairs, as Tracy sat by the crib reading an airport novel. Mom and I bent to see outside the window. The turkey, out of its cage, was performing a series of somersaults across the grass. It completed three before it hit the fence, letting out a squawk. We ran outside. It noticed us, earnestly hopping back to the side of the pen, leaned over, and began to roll over again and again.

Mom gasped. "Have you ever seen a turkey do that before?"

"Maybe it's itchy and has lice or something," I suggested.

"Heck no, they don't have hair," whispered Dad. "I know this sounds crazy, but I think it might be trying to get our attention."

"Don't be ridiculous," she replied, but continued to stare at the turkey.

It performed another series of somersaults, then hopped toward us. It stopped. A moment later, it started hopping in place, raising one wing then the other, in time to the music coming through the open window.

"Mother of pearl." Dad whistled.

He brought the turkey inside the house. At first mom objected, but Dad wasn't hearing any of it. We circled the turkey in the middle of the family room.

"Get me that ball, Sam," Dad said, pointing at the baby's red ball in the corner, next to the sofa.

I got the ball and handed it to him. Dad then rolled the ball at the turkey. It came to a rest at the turkey's clawed feet. The turkey stared at the ball, then at Dad. It ducked its head, and nudged the ball! The ball rolled up against Dad's feet. Mom laughed, started clapping her hands. Dad rolled it back. The turkey passed the ball back almost immediately.

This went on for some time.

The sun was fading behind the trees by the time Mom finally got up to make dinner. Dad placed the turkey and the red ball back in the pen. The turkey stared at me through the chicken fence. I ran upstairs and watched from behind the curtain in my bedroom as my dad went into the shed and took out the shiny new soccer ball that I'd refused to practice with all summer. He rolled it to the turkey. The turkey stared at it with its head cocked sideways for a minute. Dad looked . . . disappointed? But just as he seemed about to grab the soccer ball and toss it back in the shed, the turkey passed it back to him by kicking it with its right foot.

Mom gasped downstairs. Apparently she'd been spying on them, too. The hairs on the back of my neck shot up.

"Did everyone just see that?" Dad called out. He lightly passed the ball back to the turkey, careful not to kick it too hard, and hit the turkey with the ball. The turkey paused a few seconds, again staring at the ball, then took two hops and once again nudged the ball back to my dad with its foot.

"We're going to be filthy rich," he said. "Honey, bring out the camera. We're going to film this for *America's Funniest Home Videos*."

I watched my dad have a soccer pass with the turkey for ten minutes while my mom frantically searched for the camera downstairs. She couldn't find it, and at first Dad was angry.

"Well, we can film another time," he finally said, and looked up at me. "Sam, come down and join us."

"No, thanks," I said.

"Oh, honey," Mom said, joining Dad outside and looking up at me. "You can do it!"

"Hey, I have an idea; let's play a game of soccer," Dad suggested. "Me and Travis on one team, you and your mother on another. Here, we'll use extra shoes as goalposts."

I couldn't believe I was about to play a game of soccer with a turkey. I ambled downstairs and stood in the doorway to the backyard. "First of all, I don't want to play soccer, and second of all, I don't want to play soccer with a turkey," I said, and they sounded like two reasonable statements on my part.

"You're nervous you can't guard Travis, huh?" Dad said.

My pop was a master of psychology, at least to an eleven-year-old, and of course I couldn't help but feel jealous.

"Let's do this," I said to Mom.

"That's the spirit!" Dad pumped his fist.

For the first time in my dad's life, he saw his only son

successfully kick a soccer ball. But the triumph was short-lived. A second later Mom stole the ball from Dad and passed it up to me for an easy open-net goal, but the turkey suddenly bum-rushed me and I freaked out, remembering the time it bit my hand, and I ran blindly away from the ball and ran headfirst into a tree. Next thing I knew, I was staring up at the red and yellow leaves above me with a throbbing headache, as Mom screamed and rushed over to me. I turned to my side and saw my dad trying to high-five the turkey, shouting, "Great D!" Then he looked over at me and bragged, "You know why Travis is so tough? It's because turkeys descend from velociraptors."

"Aren't those the smaller carnivores in *Jurassic Park*? The ones who eat humans?" I asked, instantly alarmed.

Mom and Dad laughed, thinking I was being funny. And for a flicker, the turkey kind of looked over at me and made eye contact, and I swear it *licked* its beak.

Two days later. After school I walked home from the bus stop and went into the backyard. I slowly opened the back gate, making sure it didn't creak too loud. I could see the back of Tracy's head through the window in the baby's room on the top floor. I stole across the yard toward the pen. I put my hands on the top of the fence. The turkey walked out of the pen, right up to the fence. I got on my knees.

"Hi, turkey," I said.

The turkey mumbled something, leaning its head toward the fence, almost touching it. I fell back with wide eyes.

"What?" I asked.

The turkey spoke louder this time, and there was no mistaking what it said.

"DIE," it croaked.

I ran inside.

"I don't know, Martin,"Mom said into the receiver with her back to me as I passed silently through the kitchen. "Sam doesn't seem to like the turkey. . . . Give it time. Maybe he's just not into this as much as we are. . . . Thanksgiving's just around the corner. . . . Linda's not sure if she can make it. . . . Martin! It isn't nonsense. . . . He's just a child. . . ."

That night Dad tucked me into bed. Usually Mom did, but he insisted on bringing me upstairs himself. "Sam," he said, tucking and patting the comforter against my neck. "Thanksgiving's only a week and a half away, and I want you to feed the turkey in the mornings, before school. Do you think you can handle that?"

"But it talks, Dad."

"Nonsense."

"It does!" I raised my voice. "It said it wants me to die!"

Dad sighed.

"That's just your imagination," he explained. "It's because you've spent two years talking to Mr. Elizabeth all the time, so you're messed up now."

"You're wrong," I whispered. "I don't think it likes me."

He raised his voice. "You don't exactly give Travis a chance; why should he like you? You stay here in this room when I play catch with it. You stay in the kitchen when your mother and I play with it in the yard. How's this, from now on, I want you to spend a good hour each day with the turkey!" He forced himself to take a breath. "Just please try to get to know it a little better, okay? For me, Tiger?"

"Okay, Dad."

The wind pressed against the window, which was webbed with a layer of frost.

"Maybe we'll let it sleep inside tonight, in the den. It's almost freezing outside."

He switched off the light and closed the door behind him.

On Saturday afternoon my dad asked if anyone was interested in watching his old college, B.C., play football.

"Sam and I are watching a movie," Mom replied, not

taking her eyes off the TV. We were midway through a really sad movie about this woman whose husband leaves her, so she moves to a new town and meets a really nice farmer and gets a job at the local library.

"Sam, how can you be interested in that? It's a chick flick!"

"And what exactly is a chick flick?" Mom asked, staring at him.

"Um, one where nothing happens and the main character's a woman," he said. "Come on, they're playing Miami; it's a big game."

"There's another TV upstairs. You know where it is," she said, staring at the TV. "Pass the popcorn, Sam."

"Son, do you want to watch football with me? I could try explaining the rules again."

I squashed the frown forming on my face and said, "Maybe after the movie. I think she's about to get proposed to by the—"

"Oh, brother," he said, and went upstairs.

Mom and I didn't think anything of it until a couple of minutes later, when we heard heavy steps down the staircase. It didn't sound natural. I leaned back in the sofa to see. Dad was lugging the upstairs TV out into the backyard. Mom was really into the movie, so I quietly got out of my seat and went over to the kitchen and peeked out from behind the flour bowl on the counter. Dad plugged the TV into an outlet on the side of the back porch. Then he went and got two beach chairs from the shed. Then he went over to the coop and let the turkey out. My dad picked it up and set it down in one of the beach chairs before sitting down next to it. He cracked open a can of beer, and then he and the turkey began watching football together.

"What's your dad doing out there?" Mom asked during commercial break.

"He's watching football with the turkey."

"That's nice, dear," she said, her nose stuffed in an old issue of *Good Housekeeping* magazine.

I continued staring out the window at the two of them. When Dad freaked out over a great play, the turkey got all riled up and flapped its wings. Dad tried to teach it to high-five, and he even held the can of beer out to it at one point to see if it wanted a sip. It passed. My ears reddened. I was about to join him when Mom called out from the living room.

"Sam, her ex-husband showed up a few minutes ago," she said.

"Why the heck didn't you tell me?" I shouted, sprinting back into the living room.

* * *

I woke suddenly. It was two a.m. The room was blue and the night-light lay useless on the floor. Silence. I slowly panned the dark room: the desk in the corner, the Legos on the carpet, a half-finished hair salon. My legs were sweating. I closed my eyes.

Thump, thump.

The sound of footsteps on the second landing, down the hall. I sat up in bed, then immediately sank back under the covers. I peeked out at the door. The light in the hallway was on, a thin line of yellow under the crack in the door. Footsteps heading toward my room, a black shadow breaking the line of light under the door. The door slowly creaked open.

I felt feverish. The turkey stood at the edge of the room, its face silhouetted, its wings slightly askew. It stared at the bed, at me. My voice was caught in my throat. I held fistfuls of green sheets. I finally managed to whisper, "What do you want?"

"DIE," the turkey said.

"You're the one who's going to die," I cried. "We're going to eat you."

The turkey stared at me for a few seconds, then said, "DIE."

"What are you talking about? Dad's going to chop your head off, not mine."

Dad at this point was running up the steps.

"DIE," the turkey repeated.

"I swear I heard the turkey squawking— Hey, what the heck are you doing here?" Dad exclaimed. He scooped up the turkey; a feather fell to the floor.

"Sam, are you awake? Sam?"

He left the room, shutting the door tight. I shivered beneath the sheets.

The sound of the town fire alarm wailed in the distance.

My dad invited his boss, Mr. Berrian, and another coworker over for a dinner party that Friday. Mr. Berrian and his family arrived first. His son Josh was in my grade, and groaned when he saw me. Josh was the best kickball player at school, and all the guys (except me, of course) worshipped him. He was exactly the type of kid my dad wished he'd had. Naturally he hated my guts. He went straight into the living room to watch TV by himself while my dad led Mr. and Mrs. Berrian out to the backyard to meet the turkey. I stayed behind in the kitchen, feeling trapped. Then the Goldmans showed up. Dad immediately ushered them through the house to the backyard. I didn't want to be alone with Josh, so I followed them outside.

"And this is our turkey, Travis," Dad said, opening the pen. The turkey stayed put, intimidated by the strangers crowding over it.

Mr. Goldman looked at me and smiled.

"And you are?" he asked.

"I'm the son," I said softly. "Sam."

It was one thing not to get introduced to people by my parents and for them to instead introduce the turkey as if it was their son, but that weekend things got even weirder. We took the annual family photo for our Christmas cards Mom sent out every year, and Dad actually made us pose with the turkey. When the cards were ready at CVS, my mom picked them up. The card read, "Happy Holidays from the Wheatons: Martin, Grace, Sam, Baby Angie, and Travis."

In the picture, the turkey wasn't facing the camera. It had its head turned away; it was staring at *me*.

In the morning on Monday the grass in the backyard was layered with a film of white frost. My hands were shaking as I dragged the bag of seed over to the fence. I couldn't tell if they were shaking because I was scared of the turkey or because the bag was heavy. Probably both. I dug my hand in the cool, dusty bag and grabbed a handful of seeds. I sprinkled the grass on the other side of the fence. The turkey hopped out of the pen.

"DIE," it squawked.

I wondered if it was maybe my imagination, like Dad had said. Maybe it was just squawking and the creative part of my brain was turning it into words?

"Did you say 'die,' or are you just a dumb ol' turkey?" I asked.

"DIE," it repeated, taking a step toward me. There was no mistaking it; the turkey was threatening my life. I backed up slowly.

"You're not going to kill me," I said, glaring at the turkey with glazed eyes. There were bags under my eyes—I could feel them—because I'd barely slept the night before.

"DIE," it repeated, softer this time. It turned its head to the house, and seemed to sniff in the air. It could smell the eggs and bacon cooking in the kitchen. Then it looked at me again.

I gasped, realizing it wanted me to eat because it wanted to eat . . . me! I now knew its master plan. It was trying to be friendly with Dad and impress him like the pig in *Charlotte's Web* so he could trick Dad into keeping him as a pet or something, and then when the timing was right, the turkey was going to kill and eat me. I turned and quickly jumped up the steps to the porch. I reached the back door, turned to look at the turkey once more. Its head was buried in the cold grass, picking at the seeds. It looked up, its beak covered with frost and blades of green grass.

That morning at school my class drew turkeys to hang on the walls of the room. The substitute teacher handed out to the students pieces of paper with the outline of a turkey in blue ink on each sheet, along with half-used nubs of crayons. This was the type of thing we did in second grade, not fifth, but subs tended not to know how to really teach anything, so they had us draw and do little-kid things like that all the time. The girl next to me drew green wings, a purple belly. Two hearts for eyes. Josh Berrian was drawing an M16 rifle tucked under one wing. I took a red crayon out and began scratching the plastic red across the page, across the turkey's heart. I pressed the crayon against the paper so hard it ripped.

"What the heck are you doing, kid?" the substitute teacher asked. She picked up the piece of paper, examined it for a moment before balling it up and throwing it in the trash. She handed me a fresh paper. She headed to the chalkboard at the front of the room, shaking her head.

At the end of the school day I got off the bus with a headache from the chill air mixed with exhaust fumes as the bus pulled away. The Benson twins, giggling, ran off in the opposite direction. I began to walk up the street toward my house at the edge of the cul-de-sac, then stopped. I was scared to go home. The house on my left had a stone driveway. Blue chips mixed with white stones. I bent over and picked up a handful, stuffed them in my pockets for protection. I picked out a thick, jagged stone and rubbed it with my fingers.

I stopped when I got to the side of my house. Smoke rose from the chimney. The stone felt heavy in my hand. I stepped lightly over to the back entrance. Through the kitchen window, I could see my mother with her back to me, the cord of the phone wrapped around her waist. I tried to sneak in unnoticed, but the turkey stepped out of the pen. Immediately I hurled the stone at it. The stone harmlessly glanced off the roof of the pen.

It started laughing at me, I swear. Maybe to others it would've sounded like excited squawking, but it was staring at me and I knew in my heart that it was making fun of me. I was suddenly overcome with rage, something I rarely felt. My hands were shaking. I took out another stone and ran toward the fence, then threw it as hard as I could. It hit the fence and fell harmlessly to the grass. The turkey looked up at the place in the fence that I'd hit with the rock, as if to mock how off I'd been with my throw, and I seized the opportunity. I took the remaining handful and launched it at the turkey. Two or three stones pelted its belly. The turkey screamed. Mom must've seen this, because a second later she ran out the back door and collared me, lifting me off the ground with that superhuman strength you get when you find yourself trapped under a helicopter or something, like they talk about on TV.

"What on earth is your problem? I was just on the phone with your teacher. She said you ripped up everyone's Thanksgiving drawings during recess! Get inside. Your father will deal with you when he gets home from work," she snapped.

She opened the fence gate and knelt beside the turkey, cooing softly, examining its belly. She held it.

"Poor Travis. We'll fix you up, I promise."

She brought it inside the house.

"You are in a lot of trouble, son," Dad said. I shifted in my seat. The TV was on mute; the puff of smoke from the rifle without the sound looked strange to me. "Can you please tell me why you are acting like this?"

"Dad, the turkey wants to kill me," I pleaded, tears in my eyes.

"Seems like it's the other way around."

"You don't understand. It talks; it threatens me. I don't have much time. It's planning on eating me. We have to get rid of it."

"Now that's enough. You're making your mother cry. Do you actually enjoy making your mother cry? Is that what you want?"

"Don't you see what it's doing? It's trying to get on your good side because it's planning on killing me. Doesn't that mean anything to you at all?"

"You're being ridiculous. Now listen here. Your mother and I have decided to keep the turkey."

My stomach fell. Dad went on.

"We're having ham for Thanksgiving. Travis is a special animal, Sam, and you will learn to treat your brother—I mean, new pet—with respect. He just might win us some money at the state fair this spring. Now we're not going to argue about this one. You're going to have to do some growing up. If I hear about you torturing the turkey any-more, I'm going to have to really punish you. Now go to bed, and don't let me catch you with the light on."

* * *

Tracy came back on Thursday night because my parents were going out to a party. Dad searched for his keys in the family room. Tracy sat with my mom at the kitchen table, examining the beads on Mom's dress.

"They're not in the bowl, Grace," Dad said, pulling up the cushions on the sofa. He rechecked the bathroom. He came back out. The turkey squawked. The keys were resting by its clawed feet.

"Good boy, Travis!" Dad said, scratching the top of its head.

My ears boiled. The turkey smiled at me. Mom stood in the doorway and looked at me. "You can watch TV until eight thirty—that is, if you finish your homework—and then up to bed, okay, Tiger?"

They left.

Upstairs in my bedroom I tried to think of a solution to my problem, but nothing came to me. Then it dawned on me that, besides Tracy, I was basically all alone in the house with the turkey, and I felt a chill shoot down my spine. Tears rolled down my cheeks, tired tears that tickled my face. On the carpet next to me were a few feathers. I held one up above my head, let it fall. It floated down, got caught in my sweater. There were more feathers behind the chair. Suddenly I got an idea. I gathered them up, placed them in my pocket, and headed downstairs.

Tracy was in the living room, somehow listening to her headphones and talking on the phone at the same time while watching TV. The turkey sat on a pink blanket in the chair by the bookshelf. I crept back up the stairs, placing my toes against the edge of each step. I moved real slowly over the carpet, down the hallway toward the master bedroom, my ankles pressed up against the wall so I was walking sideways, like a spy breaking into a building.

I flicked the switch on the wall, and the two lamps on either side of the queen-size bed came on. I surveyed the room. The walk-in closet next to the bathroom, my mother's attempt at painting resting against the bureau. The bottles of makeup on the dresser top. I went over to the painting, held it up. A self-portrait that didn't really resemble my mother. Geese flying in the background. A yellow sun. I poked at it with my index finger. It pushed through the canvas easily. I curled my finger in the hole and pulled up. I made other holes. A piece of the painting hung over like a piece of bark.

Next I headed over to the walk-in closet. The dresses, hanging from wooden hangers in the corner, covered in plastic. I ripped those as well, making sure to rip my mother's favorite dress, the red one. It ripped easily. I made sure to damage only the bottoms of the dresses. I picked up one of my father's favorite loafers and bit into it. It tasted sour. I scuffed up the front, scratching at the leather with my fingernails.

I went back out into the bedroom, and luckily remembered at the last second to turn off the light in the closet. I listened for Tracy's footsteps but heard nothing. I opened up a green bottle on the dresser top. Inside, the liquid was thick, speckled. I lay it on the side of the dresser, and the creamy liquid spilled out onto the surface and leaked over the side, forming a puddle in the dark blue carpet.

I hopped onto their bed and kicked at the sheets. I undid the zipper on my brown corduroys. And then I peed in the middle of the mattress. I know most people would say that this was an unforgivably wrong thing to do, but the way I saw it at the time, my life was at stake. I took out the feathers, let a few drop onto the sheets, sticking to the wet mess in the middle. I stepped down quietly from the bed, careful not to make a loud sound, and took a sweeping glance at the room. The puddle of skin lotion was clotting on the carpet; beads of green liquid streaked down the side of the dresser. I placed the two remaining feathers in the middle of the room. I left the door ajar, and walked back into my bedroom.

* * *

The sound of the car pulling into the driveway. The flash of yellow across the far wall in my room. The walls shook when my dad shut the garage door. The sound of Tracy's fake laughter. The TV shut off. The sound of the turkey making excited noises. I peeked through a crack in the door and saw my mom climbing up the stairs, her high heels in her left hand. The hallway light turned on and I took a step back.

She went into the bedroom. I waited. I felt queasy with anticipation. I waited for the scream, and eventually it came. "My red dress! Martin, get up here now!" she cried. Dad raced up the stairs. He screamed, too. Now they were both screaming. I cringed, and for a moment wondered if they knew it was me. Had I left the closet light on by accident? Suddenly I couldn't remember for sure. I pictured my footprints all over the room, circles in the thick carpet. But then I heard my dad race down the steps and into the family room.

Tracy screamed, "What's wrong? Is it the baby? I stayed with her all night."

The sound of the screen door banging against the side of the house. I waited for Dad to come back inside. I could hear Mom crying at the top of the stairs. I crept over to the window and peeked out. He threw the turkey over the fence. It tumbled, and my dad shook his fist at the turkey before going back inside.

Tracy pulled away in her silver car, the sound of the engine fading in the distance. I could hear Mom and Dad whispering in the hallway. I looked outside. The turkey was in the clearing, staring up at my window. It was hopping up and down, and its beady red eyes glared up at me. I smiled down at the turkey, waved, and turned away. I climbed into bed and fell asleep almost immediately.

"Sam, come downstairs," Mom called.

I scooped up my remaining Legos and dropped them into the plastic bucket. I placed the finished Lego hair salon on the desk. Outside, the sky was bright gray. I could hear the humidifier in the baby's room hum as I walked by. Through the crack in the door, I could see the baby sleeping in her crib. The room was blue because of the night-light.

A football game on the TV in the family room, a handful of empty beer cans on the coffee table. Dad sitting on the sofa, a beer between his legs. I walked through the kitchen, and the smells of Thanksgiving hit me full force when I entered the dining room. The table was set with eight places. The baby's crib next to the window. The sound of chimes on the front stoop. Tracy and her boyfriend came in and sat next to the head of the table. I sat down next to her. The Berrians showed up and sat down on the other side of the table. Me and Josh kicked at each other under the white tablecloth—not the fun kind friends do, but more like the aggressive kind enemies do when they're forced to eat dinner together. Josh seemed surprised I was giving as much as I took. Finally, Mom and Dad sat down at opposite ends of the table.

The table was filled with almost every plate from the cupboard. Two baskets of bread, steam rising from the openings in the red cloth napkins; a bowl of store-bought slices of cranberry sauce; a glass casserole dish filled with stuffing; bowls of green peas, corn, and mashed potatoes; and at the head of the table, in front of my dad, was Travis the turkey. Everyone was staring at it. The thing practically spilled off the silver platter. It was golden brown and seemed to glow in the light.

My parents were silent amidst the idle chatter. Eventually everyone stopped talking and stared at Dad. He took a final swig of his beer and then placed the empty can on the windowsill behind him. Mom got up and took the can into the kitchen.

"Let us say grace," Dad said, bowing his head. Everyone at the table bowed their heads as well.

The baby cried.

"Bless us, O Lord, for this heavenly feast, on this day of all days, when those less fortunate than us don't—" He stopped abruptly and his face fell into his hands. The sound of my dad sobbing startled me, along with everyone else at the table. No one said anything. Dad continued to cry, and his whole body seemed to shake. Mom bent over him, embracing him from behind. She had tears in her eyes, too.

Tracy exchanged glances with her boyfriend.

It took a minute before Dad finally regained his composure. He stood up, the silver carving knife in his right hand, the three-pronged fork gently resting against the side of the turkey. Sweat rolled down the sides of the bird. The knife slowly felt its way across the side of the turkey. Dad hesitated, looked around, looked at me.

"C'mere, Sam," he said, resting the fork on the white tablecloth next to the silver platter. His voice sounded shaky.

I pushed back in my seat, walked silently over to my father's side.

"Son, I think it's time for you to learn how to carve the turkey," he said, handing me the blade.

He stepped aside.

My fists were white; the fork shook as I looked up at my dad.

"So, er, just cut on an angle down the side, use the fork for support, thin slices, slow at first—oh, man—" He turned away. The thought of cutting into poor Travis I guess was too much for him to bear in the end. Mom handed him a fresh beer. He took a long gulp, then let out a deep breath. He looked over at me and dropped the half-empty beer on the wooden floor.

I was shaving slices off the side of the turkey with the skilled ease of a seasoned butcher. It didn't seem right, given my tiny size, the way I seemed to slice through the tough skin like it was butter. I was sandwiching slices between the fork and knife, tossing them onto the plates, asking if anyone preferred dark meat. No one said a thing. I stabbed at the turkey, leaned back to pull the blade through the center. I whistled low under my breath. Turkey juice mixed with sweat on my face.

In a minute the turkey was completely carved. What remained was a skeleton of the turkey, a chunk of white meat in the shape of a rhombus. I sat down at my seat. The others stared at their plates, piled high with pieces of turkey. They began passing around the side dishes. It saddened me to see the pretty spread dissolve before my very eyes. I felt warm surrounded by my family. I smiled at my dad.

"Can we start eating, Daddy?" I asked.

"Um—okay," he replied weakly, holding the side of the

table in a vise grip. He stared down at his plate, the hairs on the white meat, the rubbery fat on the dark meat. He looked away. He couldn't eat. Neither could my mom. She stared at her plate with empty eyes, then noticed Travis's red rubber ball in the corner of the floor and shuddered. Tracy just stared at my dad in a kind of daze, and the Berrians had no idea how to act. Tracy's boyfriend took a large swallow of wine, red drops down the front of his starchy white shirt. Josh played with his green peas with a look of sheer boredom on his face as he watched them roll off the side of the table. Mr. Elizabeth winked at me, but I was too busy to wink back.

In fact, I was the only one eating.

I was swallowing pieces of turkey almost as fast as I could cut them, stopping only for a gulp of milk. It was my first time eating meat in almost two years. I tore off another piece. The sound of the knife scraping against the plate. Kernels of corn spilled off the side. My cheeks were filled, I struggled for air, but I felt like I couldn't stop. And I didn't.

And everyone else watched.

It all tasted so good, and when I looked at my dad, I was surprised to see that the expression on his face had changed, from a mixture of sadness and horror to something else entirely.

"That's my boy," he said softly.

UNACCOMPANIED MINORS

BY JEFF KINNEY

My younger brother, Patrick, is a normal, functioning adult. He has a job and a car and a house, and he's a productive member of society. Which is all pretty surprising, considering I'm the one who raised him.

Okay, so maybe that's a bit of an exaggeration. Patrick had an attentive mother and father, two older siblings, and a grandmother who made sure he was loved and cared for. But they couldn't always be there to look out for him. That's where I came in.

Once I got to babysitting age, my folks felt like they could trust me to watch my little brother for a few hours at a time while they ran errands or took care of things for the family. The moment the car pulled out of the driveway, I went to work on my defenseless kid brother.

Before you get the wrong idea, I wasn't one of those typical bullying older brothers. The damage I inflicted was mostly psychological. I was too smart to do something that would leave a mark.

Case in point: One afternoon, Patrick was happily playing a video game in the family room. This was back in the early eighties, when the Atari 2600 was all the rage. It's also when *The Smurfs* was a hugely popular Saturday morning cartoon, and Patrick was one of its disciples. The Smurfs were tiny blue men (and oddly, just one female) with white hats and no shirts (except for that female). They could often be seen walking through their valley, singing happily as they marched along in unison.

But the Smurfs had one mortal enemy: a twisted human wizard named Gargamel. Gargamel was always chasing after the Smurfs, saying, "I'll get you if it's the last thing I ever do!" I think he wanted to put the Smurfs in a cauldron and boil them. The reasons are a little hazy to me now.

Patrick was enjoying Asteroids or some such game, and I told him I needed to go out and get the mail and that he was going to be on his own for a minute or two. I walked out of the front door very casually and then booked to the backyard as fast as my feet would carry me. I got very close to the sliding glass door where Patrick was playing his game, and I spoke:

"Tra, la, la la-la-la!" I sang, as Smurflike as I could.

"I'll get you, my little Smurfs!" I shouted in my best Gargamel voice.

"Help! Papa Smurf! Save us!" I said, channeling Brainy Smurf.

Then I ran as quickly as I could to the front of the house and casually thumbed through the mail as I walked through the door. I wasn't sure if I had fooled my brother. I knew it was a long shot, and I didn't feel I had done my best Gargamel.

But when I walked into the family room, Patrick was standing bolt upright. The joystick was lying on the ground, and on the TV were the words "Game Over."

Patrick was as white as a ghost. His eyes were wide, and he looked absolutely stricken with fear.

"What's wrong?" I asked innocently.

Patrick gulped, and a single word escaped his lips.

"*Smurfs!*" he gasped.

The Smurfs incident wasn't the first time I blurred the line between fantasy and reality for Patrick, and it wouldn't be the last.

When I was a kid, I loved milk. I drank almost a gallon a day. Patrick, on the other hand, despised milk. Looking back, he was probably lactose intolerant, and I'm sure milk upset his stomach.

But I made it my personal mission to make Patrick love milk just as much as I did. After all, "Milk builds strong bones!" the ads on TV told us. I wanted to make sure my younger brother had strong bones, just like me.

Reason didn't work on Patrick, and neither did bribery. So I tried lying, and that did the trick.

I created a lie so elaborate that I came to half believe it myself. I convinced Patrick that he was a superhero named Shazaam and that he needed milk to fuel his powers. Why couldn't he fly or jump over tall buildings? Why, it was because he wasn't drinking enough milk.

And why hadn't Mom and Dad told Patrick he was a superhero? Why, because every superhero has a secret identity, and his was so secret, even his mother and father didn't know about it.

So under my supervision, Patrick choked down glass upon glass of milk. He was frustrated that he didn't yet have X-ray vision or the ability to fly, but I patiently explained that his powers would come to him if he just drank more milk.

The lie grew bigger and bigger over time. I'm certain

that Patrick was having a hard time keeping his secret identity under wraps in kindergarten, where he had to sing the ABCs and finger paint with the mere mortals who were his classmates.

But every superhero has a weakness, and Patrick's kryptonite was the rocket slide at the town park. The rocket slide was made up of a tower with a ladder running through the center of it and a metal spiral slide that wrapped around it. Patrick was absolutely terrified of that slide, just as I was when I was a kid. He wouldn't get within fifty feet of that thing.

So I convinced Patrick that by climbing that ladder, all of the powers that were promised to him would be bestowed when he reached the top. He would be able to fly, to see with X-ray vision, and to finally get his Shazaam suit. Plus, as a kicker, he'd get a Shazaam action figure. All he needed to do was to conquer his fears and climb that ladder.

Still, Patrick was skeptical. It took weeks of convincing before Patrick finally stepped inside the tower and began the long climb up the ladder. Little did he know, I was right behind him.

When Patrick got to the top, the sky did not part and he was not transformed into a being with superpowers. Not even an action figure in sight.

There was just an older brother who pushed him down the slide, headfirst.

The superhero scam ended in that moment, and I'm sure many dreams died for Patrick on that day. I can't imagine the psychological damage that occurs when you've spent a year living a secret identity as a superhero with no actual powers only to find that it was all a lie. All I know is, to this day, Patrick won't go near a glass of milk.

The Shazaam story was a big lie, but there were lots of smaller ones along the way.

In the early eighties, a marvelous new technological wonder called the "VCR" started appearing in homes. The VCR allowed you to watch movies on your TV when you wanted to—an incredibly novel concept at the time.

Picking out a movie from the video rental place was a big deal. We weren't especially well-off, so as a family, we were very careful about which film we brought into our house on a Saturday night. We took turns choosing, and on this night, it was Patrick's turn to pick.

Patrick wanted to rent *Meatballs*, a raucous comedy about summer camp, which was a big hit of the day. But I had already seen it, so I wanted him to pick something else.

Patrick wasn't budging. So I convinced him that *Meatballs*

was the most boring movie ever created. I told him that the whole film consisted of a single shot of two cold meatballs sitting on a shelf. Nothing happened in the movie at all, I explained. Just ninety minutes of two lifeless clumps of meat.

Unfortunately for me, this struck Patrick as a really entertaining concept. He rented the movie anyway. I think Patrick was confused and maybe even a little disappointed when he realized that there was more to the movie than I had described.

And speaking of meatballs . . .

One night, I was responsible for feeding Patrick dinner. The instructions from Mom were pretty clear: There's left-over spaghetti in the refrigerator, so take out the bowl, put some spaghetti on a plate, and put cellophane wrap over it. Heat in the microwave for a minute and a half and serve.

Only I skipped that last step, just for fun. I called Patrick to the dinner table and put his plate of spaghetti in front of him. I told him to be careful, because the spaghetti was very hot.

So Patrick stabbed a meatball with a fork and blew on it for a while to cool it down. Then he took a bite.

I remember seeing all of the muscles in Patrick's face go slack as the ice-cold meatball fell from his mouth back onto his plate. And if you ever wondered why Patrick isn't a big fan of leftovers, now you know.

It might not surprise you that over time, Patrick developed a deep suspicion and even a dislike of me. He looked for every chance to get one over on me, and I used that to my advantage.

When Patrick was in the fifth grade, he became a huge fan of professional wrestling. This was when the people involved in professional wrestling swore their sport was "real." I spent hours trying to convince Patrick that it was all staged, but he tuned me out. He was convinced that the blood feud between Hulk Hogan and André the Giant was the real deal, and there was nothing I could do to break the spell.

Professional wrestlers sport giant, ornate title belts when they win their weight division. Patrick and his fifth-grade friends wanted to be like Hulk Hogan, so they formed an arm-wrestling circuit at their school and made an impressively elaborate title belt out of construction paper. The thing was a real work of art.

Patrick beat out his classmates to claim the title, and he brought the belt home with him. He proudly displayed his belt on a shelf in his bedroom.

When I saw it, I knew it had to be mine.

So I said, "Patrick, do you think I'm immature?"

"Yeah!" he said, happy to criticize me.

"Do you think I act my age, or do I act younger?" I said.

"Younger!" he said, really getting into it.

"Would you say I act like . . . a fifth grader?" I asked meekly.

"YEAH!" he said happily.

"Would you say I *am* a fifth grader?" I asked.

"YEAH! Ha-ha!" he laughed.

"Okay," I said. "Wanna arm wrestle?"

"Sure," Patrick said, not at all phased by the turn in the conversation.

We arm wrestled. I beat him. I relieved him of his fifth-grade arm-wrestling belt. To Patrick's credit, he didn't contest the results.

I didn't always come out on top. Patrick got in his licks, and once or twice, he got the best of me.

One of those times was when Patrick was about seven years old. He wanted to watch *He-Man* on TV and I wanted to watch a show with music videos. These were the days before people had multiple televisions in their houses, and the family room was a battlefield.

There was no question as to who was going to win in this case. I had the muscle, and Patrick was no match for me. I turned the knob on the TV to the channel with the music videos, then I went to get myself a snack from the laundry room (which is where, for some reason, my mom kept the junk food).

The second I stepped into the laundry room, I heard a click behind me. Patrick had locked me into the laundry room by sliding a chain across the door. I could open the door a crack . . . just enough to see Patrick turn the channel back to *He-Man* and settle onto the couch.

As Patrick got older, he started getting wise to my lying. He even started telling some lies of his own. That's when things got pretty confusing, and we both realized we needed a failsafe way of knowing when the other guy was telling the truth.

So we started using the word "honest" as our bail-out word. Let me explain.

Let's say I told Patrick he had to wear pajamas to school because it was pajama day. He might say, "Really?" And I'd say, "Yep."

And then he'd say, "Are you lying?" and I'd say, "Nope."

But then he'd say, "Honest?" Only it was really drawn out, like this: "*Honnnnnest?*"

And that would break me. I'd fess up and tell him the truth, sparing him the humiliation of going to school in his footie pajamas.

I don't know how that word became such a powerful truth serum between us. All I know is that it became an unbreakable oath, and neither of us ever dared to lie once that word was uttered. Using the "honest" card was like asking you to swear on your mother's life. It became a sacred trust.

One summer, Patrick went to a friend's for a sleepover. The kid's name was Andrew, and he was some sort of super-genius. He was the kind of kid who could build a working robot.

Patrick returned from the overnight with a stunning tale. He said that Andrew had built a working laser cannon, just like the ones in the Star Wars films. Andrew had tossed a tennis ball in the air and fired the laser at it, blowing the ball to bits.

I didn't believe Patrick. I peppered him with questions about the details. What color was the laser beam? How long was the blast? What kind of sound did it make? And why did Andrew's mother allow Andrew to create a danger-ous weapon in his bedroom?

But Patrick parried my questions with detailed answers.

The laser beam was green. The blast was about the length of his arm. It made a loud sound, but Andrew had stuffed pillows under the door so his parents wouldn't know what he was up to.

And there was more. The laser beam had left a scorch mark on the wall, which Andrew had covered up by moving his dresser in front of it.

I was pretty certain that this was all a lie, but it was a very detailed, well-thought-out lie. All of the pieces were there, and Andrew was a genius after all, so who knew what kind of things he could build?

I needed to know the truth, so I played the only card I had.

"Honest?" I asked Patrick.

He paused for a very long time, then looked me square in the eye and said, in a somber voice, "Honest."

That affirmation completely rocked my world. Suddenly, everything I'd seen in science fiction movies was possible. Andrew could build a laser cannon. Could he build one for me? And if he could do that, could he create the Holy Grail of laser weapons: a light saber?

My mind raced. How could we protect Andrew from the government goons who would surely descend on his house and take his experiments away? This laser cannon had to remain a secret. And most important, how could we profit from this invention? We were going to be rich . . . I was sure of it.

As the weeks went by, I tried to set up a time when I could see Andrew's laser cannon in person. But Patrick was very elusive and noncommittal. He didn't seem to be able to arrange for an in-person demonstration of this fantastic weapon.

Finally, Andrew came to our house for a sleepover. Patrick was acting strangely, as if he didn't want me to talk to Andrew face to face. But finally, I got a moment alone with him.

"When can I see your laser cannon?" I whispered to him in a feverish tone.

"My what?" he said.

"Your laser cannon!" I said, a little impatient.

But Andrew was being coy. He was playing dumb, which I had to concede was a pretty good strategy given the nature of the weapon.

I pressed on. "Listen, I know you built a laser cannon in your bedroom and that you blasted a tennis ball to smithereens with it. And I know all about the blast mark on your wall and how you covered it up with a dresser. I'm not going to tell anyone about it, so don't worry."

Andrew stared at me blankly. Man, he was good. By this time, Patrick had entered the room, and he was acting very skittish.

Then Andrew spoke. "I don't have a laser cannon. Are you talking about my tennis ball shooter? I made something that can fling a tennis ball across the room."

So now I knew. There was no laser cannon. All of the excitement that I had stored up was drained in an instant. Patrick had a sheepish grin. In terms of lying, the student had surpassed the teacher.

I had to respect him for that, but still, he had broken the sacred oath. Had he not uttered the unbreakable oath? Had he not said, "Honest"?

I was furious. I marched upstairs to my mother's room with Patrick nipping at my heels. He begged me not to tell on him, not to expose him as a liar.

I burst into my mom's bedroom. She was on the phone. I didn't give a second thought to interrupting her.

"Mom!" I said as she put her hand over the phone, annoyed.

"Patrick told me Andrew built a laser cannon, and he said 'HONEST'!" I exclaimed, fully expecting her to drop the phone in horror.

I thought that a grounding was in order. Six months was

reasonable. No snacks, no TV, no video games: That would just about do it.

"So what?" said Mom.

I admit I tormented my younger brother growing up, but if you ask me, I did him a favor. As an adult, Patrick is the least jumpy person I know, and I take full credit for that.

When we were kids, I would scare my brother every chance I got. Any time there was an opportunity to jump out of a closet, or hide behind the shower curtain, or emerge suddenly from the furnace room, I was there.

One time when Patrick was very young, I spent about an hour in the basement hiding behind a half wall as he played merrily with his *Star Wars* characters on the other side. I was a very patient hider, all the better to surprise my prey.

I found some masking tape and rolled it in a perfect, slow arc around the half wall to where Patrick was playing with his action figures. The roll of tape came to a rest right in front of him.

There was a long period of silence as Patrick tried to make sense of how a roll of masking tape might have moved across the floor all on its own. I think he came to the conclusion that a ghost was responsible.

"MOMMMMMMMMM!" Patrick yelled.

"RAHHHRRRRR!" I screamed, leaping up from my hiding place. Patrick just about jumped out of his skin.

But this was a rare victory for me. Over the years, Patrick became more and more immune to my scare tactics. Even my best-executed screams and sudden appearances seemed to elicit less and less of a reaction over time. Finally, when Patrick was a teenager, it became impossible for me to get any kind of response at all.

We had a deck on the back of the house, and my parents installed a hot tub. Before they filled it with water, I asked my father to help me to pull a prank on Patrick. It was a cold winter night, and I climbed into the empty hot tub and had my father put the heavy cover over me. Then my father went inside the house and asked Patrick to help lift the cover off of the hot tub.

From where I was hiding, I could hear the muffled sounds of my father and brother approaching. As soon as they lifted the cover off of the hot tub, I sprang out and screamed like a cat whose tail had been run over by a truck.

I was sure that this prank would be enough to scare anyone half to death. Even my father, who was in on the trick, was startled. But I got no response out of Patrick at all. Nothing. He might as well have been doing his taxes.

That's when I realized that trying to scare him was hopeless. I haven't even tried in all the years since.

A few minutes after I pulled the hot tub trick, Patrick's friend, a big football player named Mike, came to our house. I quickly got my father and my brother to put the cover back over me to see if we could scare Mike.

I did the same thing, leaping out of the hot tub and screaming. This time, the trick worked. I think I nearly scared Mike to death. He hyperventilated over the side of the deck for about fifteen minutes, trying to catch his breath. So at least that proved the trick itself was a good one. Just not good enough to scare Patrick.

Even today, Patrick is always calm, and nothing really seems to rattle him. I just hope he knows he has his big brother to thank for that.

Sadly, all good things come to an end. Over time, the abuse I heaped upon Patrick ended, and we became more like peers. Or maybe just more like normal brothers.

Of course, brothers can still be rivals, and each of us needed a way to prove supremacy over the other. And just as we came up with a sacred trust in the word "honest," we came up with a competition that was based on honor, sportsmanship, and a stuffed lion.

The name of the game was Last Licks, and I believe it's one of the purest games ever invented. It took us years to develop the rules of the game and create a perfect, balanced sport. I won't be surprised if one day Last Licks becomes an official Olympics event.

Here are the rules of Last Licks. You start with an agreed-upon projectile. For us it was a mangy, stuffed lion that belonged to our dog, Woofie. The object can't be too hard or too soft. You have to be able to bean it at someone's head without causing too much damage.

You also need a dog for this game, and if you don't have one, I'm afraid you're out of luck. Cat people need not apply.

Last Licks starts with someone pegging the other with the projectile. That's the official start of the game. It doesn't matter if the other person is watching TV, reading a magazine, or eating. They need to stop what they're doing and engage in the game.

When the person who threw the projectile hits his target, he then taunts the other person by saying, "Last Licks!" and making his forefinger and thumb into an L. He then flips the L back and forth, preferably saying, "LL!" in an annoying fashion.

If the other person does not reciprocate or engage in the

game, the taunting continues. This can go on for days if necessary.

The next step is for the person who has been hit to throw the projectile back at the original attacker. Here's where the rules become more complicated.

If the person throwing the projectile hits his mark, he now has "Last Licks" and can do some taunting of his own. If, however, the other person catches the projectile, the hit doesn't count. The person who caught the projectile has five seconds to place the projectile on the ground so the thrower can recover it. If the catcher does not cough up the projectile in five seconds, then it's as good as if he had been hit.

Here's where the dog comes into play. By this time in the game, the dog is excited that his stuffed animal is being thrown around and is watching it like a hawk. If the stuffed animal lands or is placed on the ground, the dog is likely to snatch it up and run away. This is where the game gets fun. The person with "Last Licks" can taunt the opposing player as the opposing player tries to chase down the dog with the projectile in its mouth.

The perfect move in Last Licks is when you throw the projectile at the opposing player's head, it bounces off, and the dog catches it and runs away. There's really nothing better than that. It's like pulling off a perfect McTwisty 1260 on a snowboard.

So how do you win at Last Licks? It can't go on forever, of course. There has to be a winner and a loser.

The game ends when your dad wakes up and comes downstairs. See, Last Licks is always played late at night, in the family room, right underneath your parents' bedroom. And something always happens to wake Dad up. You knock over a lamp, you break a piece of glass, the dog starts barking uncontrollably—something *always* happens to wake Dad up. And when Dad comes downstairs to give you a piece of his mind, the game is over, and whoever has Last Licks wins for the night.

Like I said, it's a perfect game. It was honed over years of play testing, rule changing, and waking up Dad. And I'm proud to say that over time, I netted the most wins. I was awesome at bouncing the lion off of Patrick's head and landing it right in Woofie's mouth.

Of course, we couldn't stay kids forever. Patrick and I each went off to college, came back to stay with Mom and Dad for a bit, then moved out. But shortly before our parents sold the house we grew up in, Patrick and I found ourselves hanging out in the family room and talking about old times.

I spotted a ragged-looking tail underneath the couch. Could it be . . . the stuffed lion?

We played one last rowdy game of Last Licks. And although my opponent battled fiercely, by the time Dad came downstairs and the dust had settled, I can proudly say I was the winner.

Honest.

"WHAT? YOU THINK *You* GOT IT ROUGH?"
BY CHRISTOPHER PAUL CURTIS

My gramps, Papa Red, has been living with us for a year now and is straight-up nuts. I don't say that because the man can't understand anything that was invented after the wheel, either. I say that because one day I'm gonna be a writer and I've trained myself to be real observant. As part of doing research for my upcoming autobiography I've read a bunch of issues of *Modern Psychology* and now, instead of wanting to knock Papa Red the mess out, I understand that he can't help himself. The magazines say it's all understandable why he lost his mind: it's because of *his* father, Iron John, a man who was so far off the deep end he was at the bottom of the ocean.

Papa Red knew, kind of, what it was that had drove him nuts, too. Man, I'd be neighbors with Oprah Winfrey if I had a dollar for every time in the past twelve months he told me and my worthless brother, Chester, something like, "What? You little chumps think you got it rough? Y'all little momma's boys ain't got no idea what rough is. When I was your age my old man was so rough on me and my brothers and sisters that . . ." Then you fill in the blanks with any story that involves torturing children right up to the point of death.

It was Monday and my turn to sit with Papa Red. I got to his bedroom door and Chester was standing just inside the doorway.

Great. I was just in time to hear Gramps's latest "had it so rough" story.

He was saying to Chester, "That ain't nothing. My daddy was so rough on us that he'd hang us upside down from the clothesline and smear honey on our faces and wouldn't cut us down until the crows had come and plucked our eyes out! You hear me, boy? You got any idea how it feels to be dangling from a clothesline waiting for a crow to come pluck your eyes out? Sometimes the crows wouldn't show up for days! Days, I'm saying! And not every crow in the world likes the taste of honey, neither, so you just hung there and waited until one with a sweet tooth flew by. And you best not try to wiggle off that clothesline or when Iron John caught hold of you he'd *really* put you on punishment! Now that's being rough!"

I rolled my eyes and shook my head. Chester, who I already told you is a certified moron, had to point out the obvious, "But Papa Red, I'm looking at your eyes right now. How'd you get 'em back from the crow?"

Papa Red was real old-school, and back talk and sass like that always lead him to violence, and even though he's stuck sitting in his wheelchair he can still do some damage if you aren't careful. Right after you'd sass him he'd say something like, "Huh? I didn't quite catch that, you know. I ain't hearing good as I used to." Then he'd try to distract you by cupping his left hand around his ear all the while reaching down with his right hand to grab hold of what he called his licking stick, hoping he could lure you a little closer.

One thing you gotta say about Chester is that he isn't extremely dumb. He'd seen how far the switch had reached the last time he got whacked and knew right where to stand so it couldn't get him again.

He said, "So I gotta ask, how're you seeing me if a crow ate your eyes?"

He snapped his fingers, "Oh, I got it! Those are glass eyes you're looking at me with. Could you pull one of 'em out for me so's I can see how they work?"

Papa Red got his hand around the switch and said, "Sure, boy, come here and let me put it in your hand. I don't wanna take a chance and drop it and have it break. These things is expensive."

Chester laughed and said, "Naw, Gramps, why don't you just roll it to me? You know, like a marble."

I know it's not possible, but when Papa Red whipped that switch from beside his wheelchair it was glowing and making a humming sound. He slapped it across his palms twice.

"Aww, you done slipped up now," Papa Red said. "I got you and your back-talking, sass-filled little mouth right where I want you! I'm like a spider what's set a trap and you ain't nothing but a juicy fly!"

Chester checked the spot on the carpet where he knew the switch could reach, and just to be safe, took another half step back. He laughed and said, "Yeah, well, you're gonna have to postpone your dinner reservation, Spiderman. This fly's gotta buzz off to handle some of his business."

Papa Red raised the switch over his head.

Chester was feeling real sassy. He laughed and said,

"What you gonna do with that stick, old man? Huh? What?"

A huge mistake.

Papa Red said, "What'm I gonna do with this stick? I'm gonna smote you, that's what. And I know you ain't got no idea what that word means, so I'm gonna demonstrate, and I'll bet by the end of this demonstrating 'smote' is one word you won't soon be forgetting."

When the tip of that glowing, humming switch caught Chester's shoulder I wished I had a video camera 'cause his expression would've got me a million hits on YouTube! The first thing he did was get a stupid, shocked look on his face, then he howled, then he jumped straight up and made another huge mistake: instead of running to the door he grabbed his shoulder and backed into a corner.

Papa Red didn't even have to move his wheelchair. He sat there and commenced wailing on Chester from ten feet off! The way he was swinging that switch, Papa Red looked like a conductor from the Flint Symphony Orchestra waving a baton during some big, busy, rushy song like Beethoven's Ninth. Every time the switch hit Chester it would go, "*Pie-ow!*" and Chester would yelp like a Chihuahua.

I know I should've tried to stop Papa Red but the way that switch was ripping through the air, I figured I didn't want to be any part of what they call "collateral damage." Besides, Chester *is* a certified moron and deserved this for always messing with Papa Red. What did that dude on that old TV show used to say? "Don't do the crime if you can't do the time."

Chester didn't have a clue how Papa Red was able to hit him with the switch, but I knew what had happened. Chester isn't the only one who's certified in our family. Our little sister, Lulu, is certified, too, but she's a certified snitching, butt-kissing little brat, and she does everything Papa Red asks.

Yesterday I'd seen her going into his room carrying a tape measure and a saw. When I asked her what she was doing she told me, "You don't look like my momma. Don't be questioning me. I got rights. . . ." Then she sashayed her trash-talking little behind into Gramps's room.

A couple of seconds later they both came out, her riding on the back of his wheelchair as they whirred to the front door. The saw and tape measure were in his lap.

I didn't care, but just trying to be sociable, I'd asked, "Where you going, Papa Red?"

He stopped the chair, looked at me, and said, "My momma died in nineteen hundred and thirty-seven, and she was a smart woman. If she was gonna get reincarnated in someone else's body I don't think she'd choose the body of a ten-year-old pimply idiot like you. So less'n you got some ID that shows that she's took over your body, I'm gonna ignore that question and any others that come outta that crooked-tooth mouth of yours."

It's sad but the only thing he said that wasn't true was that I'm ten years old. I'm really nearly fourteen. Oh, I'm also not an idiot.

Lulu stuck her tongue out at me.

Papa Red shifted the wheelchair back in gear and they rolled out the front door.

It all made sense now: Papa Red had measured how long a switch he'd need to cover the whole room and taken Lulu and the saw out to find one that was long enough!

Like I said, he's nuts, but he sure ain't stupid.

Momma must've heard the crack of six or seven "Pie-ow"s and six or seven of Chester's screams before she finally came to see what the commotion was about. She's not as worried about collateral damage as I am and took two good whacks before she snatched the switch away from Papa Red.

"Daddy! I told you you can't be beating these children like that. This is the twenty-first century. We don't do that anymore."

Papa Red laughed and said, "Call the po-po on me, then. I'm ninety years old. I'll just tell 'em I was having a twentieth-century flashback! You baby them boys too much, and that one's got a real fresh mouth."

Momma snapped the licking stick in half.

Gramps said, "I want to move back to Gary. They know how to treat spoiled brats there."

Momma said, "No one's moving nowhere. This is your home now and I need you to look after these children while I'm at work. How can I leave you in charge if everything leads to you whipping them? Besides, where on earth are you getting these switches from anyway?"

Lulu would've busted me in a heartbeat. I kept quiet.

Papa Red said, "My lips are sealed, beat me if you want but I ain't talking. The Kenyans captured me back in '52 and worked me over for two weeks and couldn't even get my social security number from me. You think you can make me talk? Ha! You and these two little momma's boys ain't got nothing on the Kenyans."

Momma said, "Papa, I told you a million times the United States has never been at war with the Kenyans."

"That's what makes them so dangerous. No one knows how tricky they are."

Momma sighed and said, "Chester, Trevor, follow me."

Momma closed Papa Red's bedroom door and we stood in the hallway. Chester wiped his tears and sniffled while I waited to see what mind game Momma was gonna play on us next.

Chester said, "I'm calling child protection on him."

Momma said, "You aren't calling anybody. I don't know what you did, but I know you provoked him."

She put her hands on our shoulders and said, "Boys, this can't keep happening. I need you to look after your grandfather, not rile him up."

Unbelievable! Once again she was gonna try to blame me for what Chester did.

I said, "But Momma, I didn't do—"

She squeezed my shoulder, "Trevor, you're the oldest, I need you to keep things in order here when I go to work."

"But Momma!"

"But nothing. You know Papa's homesick and a little confused some of the time. You have to do everything you can to make him comfortable being with us. Trevor, I need you to be mature here."

"But that's not fair! You *know* I'm not mature!"

"Then you're going to have to pretend you are. Isn't it your day to keep him company? Get in there and be nice to him. He's led an interesting life; if you give him a chance

195

he's got lots of great stories he can share with you."

"They might be interesting to you, but I got a life; to me they're—"

The gentle hand on my shoulder turned into an eagle's claw. "Get in there *now*!"

What could I do? I'm in the ninth grade. I need food and clothes and stuff and she's the dictator in control of everything.

Papa Red was a mean old fart, but it was sort of easy to understand why. A little over a year ago him and his older sister and his younger brother had their own place in Gary, Indiana. Even though they were old as water, they did everything for theirselves.

They were cool until his baby brother, Herbert, who was eighty-eight years old, got forcibly retired off the railroad. They gave him a big party and a clock. The newspapers in Gary obviously don't have much to write about; they took his picture and wrote a story about him. Papa Red kept the newspaper article folded in his wallet. Three weeks after he retired great uncle Herbert dropped dead in the kitchen.

A week after his funeral great-aunt LaWanda went down to Lake Michigan and sat on a park bench and froze herself to death.

The day after that we borrowed a car and drove to Gary

and brought Papa Red back to live with us in Flint. Kicking and fighting the whole way. But Momma works in a nursing home and said there wasn't any way in the world her father was going in one.

I knocked on the old man's door. "Papa Red, can I come in for a minute?"

He thought I was Chester. He yelled, "What? You back for more? Sure, come on in."

His chair was still next to the window and he had his right hand by his side. He probably had a spare switch.

I put my hands up in front of me. "Look, Papa Red, I didn't say nothing smart-mouth to you. It was Chester."

He showed his right hand. All he had in it was his house slipper. Cool. He couldn't dish out too much pain with that.

I sat on the edge of his bed and tried to think of the best way to start a conversation with this crazy old man.

All I could think of was, "So, the Kenyans captured you, huh?"

"Yeah, I let that slip, didn't I? Well, nice try, but you ain't getting another word outta me about that. Now, let's get serious. How much you gonna charge me to go out and cut me a switch that's exactickly eight feet, three and a quarter inches long?"

"You'll have to wait for Lulu to do that. I ain't getting involved."

"For the love of…. If your great granddaddy Iron John got reincarnated and saw how washed out and weak his genes had got over the years he'd wanna die all over again."

I don't have any idea at all why the man was so stuck on talking about reincarnation all the time. I told him, "I don't care what you say, Papa Red. There's no way your father was rougher on you and your brothers and sisters than Momma is on us."

"What? You think *you* got it rough? Let me tell you about rough."

Here we go, but this is what Momma wanted me to do to earn my room and board, so I acted like I was interested.

"It was back in thirty-five, two years before Momma died. I was 'bout your age, ten years old."

"Papa Red, you know I'm thirteen."

"Well, if that's true I wouldn't let no one know, 'cause you act like you're ten. Interrupt me again and I'll wear you out with this house shoe. Nineteen hundred and thirty-five. Gary, Indiana, where it *really* gets cold in the wintertime, not this little chill y'all here in Flint whine about."

I wasn't looking for a weather report so I told him, "You were saying Iron John was rough on you?"

He said, "If you keep your mouth shut and listen you wouldn't have to ask what I was saying. Gary, Indiana, nineteen hundred and thirty-five, middle of the winter. At that time in the Depression there were only three black people in all of Chicago that owned a Packard automobile. Your great granddad Iron John was the only one in the entire state of Indiana who did."

"What, was a Packard expensive, like a Benz?"

"Expensive? Your great granddad's cost more than three Cadillacs. For thirty years he used to be chauffeur for Mr. Tom Foster, who ran one of the mills in Gary. When old man Foster died, 'stead of leaving Iron John some cash he willed him that Packard. It was in all the papers, too. I got the articles to prove it.

"Main problem with that Packard was it didn't have no desire at all to start up once it got below zero outside. Iron John was 'bout the only one who could get it running. That's why when I wasn't but ten years old he started teaching me 'bout starting it in the cold. It just got to be one more chore I had to be ready to do morning, noon, or night.

"I know this here happened on a Friday night around six o'clock 'cause that was spaghetti night and another one of my chores was to fix the spaghetti with Ma. We already'd

199

mixed the tomato paste and tomato sauce and onions and green peppers and garlic and I was cutting up the hot dogs and dropping them into the pot of the burbling-up sauce.

"Most folks think when you make spaghetti all you do is hack up some weenies and toss them any old which way into the pot. Sure, you'll end up with something close to spaghetti if you do that but will it be any good? Will someone be so impressed that they'll stop eating for a second, look up, and say, "My goodness, that boy sure can cook"? I don't think so.

"Life's all about learning tricks, and one of the tricks in making the kind of spaghetti that someone *might* say is righteous good is to cut the hot dogs at a forty-five-degree angle, not straight across. That lets more of the sauce soak up into the meat and gives it that little pop of flavor everyone likes so much when they bite into one. Most people don't know that when Chinese folks invented spaghetti they used to peel the skin clean off the hot dog. Not that they had anything against the skin. They did it so they could get the most sauce soaked into each piece of hot dog."

Papa Red looked at me and said, "I know you wants to be a writer, but if you had any sense you'd be taking notes."

I tapped the side of my head. "I got a real good memory, Papa Red."

He told me, "I like keeping my cooking as original as I can, so I tried peeling the skin off the hot dogs once, and I ain't trying to talk no smack about the way Chinese folks cook, but it didn't work for me. After I peeled the hot dogs I ended up with a pile of meat skins that looked pretty disgusting, and with that reddish brown color, my brother, Herbert, said it looked like me and Iron John, who was a redbone like me, had shed all the skin off our fingers and toes and set them in a nasty, flimsy pile. Besides, taking the skin off took that magic little pop away and everyone complained that they weren't getting as much meat. But what's life if you don't try new things?"

Papa Red was getting off the subject again. I wanted to hear about that Packard and this was turning into the Rachael Ray show. "Papa Red, you were telling me about starting that old car."

He didn't miss a beat. "Ma had been at the sink washing dishes and I'd cut half the hot dogs up and was plopping the bits into the spaghetti sauce one at a time so's not to splash no sauce on the stove. The back door come open and a wind so cold that you'da swore God was mad at the world cut through the heat of the kitchen. Next thing you know, a *real* angry god, this one the god of five forty-one Jackson Street, aka Iron John, come in from outside.

"He said, 'What the heck is this? I thought I told you 'bout teaching that boy this woman mess. If he's gonna be a man you can't have him sitting in the kitchen cooking. If you too lazy to do it your own self get one of those worthless girls to help you.'

"He grabbed one of the whole hot dogs from the butcher's paper next to me and said, 'Get your coat on, boy.' Then, just to meddle with Ma, he left the back door open as he went back out.

"In my mind I imagined myself taking the knife and sticking it into his hand so hard that he'd be pinned to the kitchen table. Then I'd calmly reach over, take the stolen hot dog out of his hand, and tell him, 'Touch another one of my hot dogs when I'm cooking, and next time it'll be your tongue I stab to the table.'

"Ma picked up the dishrag to wipe her hands, closed the door, and told me, 'You best go on,' and took the knife to finish cutting the hot dogs.

"I said, 'You know you got to cut them sidewa—'

"She swatted at me with the dish towel and said, 'Look, Chef Boyardee, I been doing this since before you was born. Now you best get out there and see what he wants before he gets mad.'

"When I got dressed for the cold and went outside the

car wasn't running and Iron John was sitting inside behind the steering wheel. The battery must be dead.

"I wondered why he wanted me to come with him and opened the big Packard's back door, but before I could crawl in, Iron John said, 'Naw, sit up front.' I opened Momma's door and slid into the car.

"He told me, 'It's 'bout time you learned some man-work. I ain't 'bout to let no one turn my little men-boys into no little bouquet of flowers.'

"I said, 'Yes, sir,' and something in my stomach twisted a little when I wondered what 'man-work' was. I hoped it wasn't gonna be something too terrible.

"He pointed the hot dog he stole like a finger. I had to smile at myself 'cause, just like Herbert had told me, it *was* right close to the same reddish color as his skin, which I guess means it was the same color as mine, too. He started the man-work lesson by wagging the hot dog and saying, 'You know this here is the top of the line auto-mobile for the Packard Motor Car Company, right?'

"'Yes, sir,' I said.

"'And how many colored folks in Chicago or the whole state of Indiana owns one of these Packard auto-mobiles?'

"I'd heard it a million times. I said, 'Two doctors and one numbers man in Chicago and only you in Indiana.'

"'That's right. And it's 'bout time you learned how to start a man's car up in the winter. Ain't no reason for me to be dragging my bad leg out in the cold to warm this car up when I got you and your worthless ma sitting 'round doing nothing.'

"This was a lie. He always made every last one of us come out into the car when he warmed it up. He told us a long time ago that starting the car on a cold day made him miserable. He also was always telling us he was a expert on white people and that one of the best sayings they'd ever come up with was 'misery needs company,' and when it came to being froze in the winter he couldn't think of no one to be better company for his misery than Ma and his kids.'"

Papa Red looked back out the window.

After a minute he said, "Iron John stopped using the hot dog as a pointer and broke it in half. For a second, I thought he was gonna give me one of the halves, but I should've known better. He started eating from the broke-off end of one of the pieces and kept the other one tight in his hand.

"Sure, I wondered why he started eating a hot dog from the middle like that, who wouldn't, but there's some things that you don't wanna drag out by asking questions.

"I still didn't say nothing when he ate everything on both hot dogs except the tips then set the two little round pieces of meat on the dashboard.

Papa Red said, "Iron John pointed at the glove box. I opened it and looked back at him.

"'Reach me that,' he said.

"There was some papers, some tools, and a half-froze can of something. I dug all the tools out of the glove box and set them on the seat between us.

"'That there can, too.' He kept his hand out.

"It was one of them aerosol cans. It had Starting Fluid writ 'cross the top. I gave it to him. He lifted his jacket, sweater, and undershirt and put the icy can right on his chest.

"I know, but remember I wasn't 'bout to keep this man-work lesson going one second more by asking questions.

"He said, 'You see the suffering I go through for you brats?'

"I didn't see nothing, but I knew the words he was looking for. 'Yes, sir.'

"The car-starting lesson got real complicated but I was on top of it. He showed me how to open the hood and loosen the air cleaner off the carburetor and why he had to use his body heat to warm the starting fluid so it would unfreeze and spray and how much to pull the choke out and how long to wait if the car didn't fire up after the first try. To finish off the lesson he explained to me when the proper time was to tromp on the gas and when to ease off the ignition.

"That had been a good day for the Packard and it fired up on the first try. Iron John slapped the dashboard and said, 'You ain't gonna be this good at it but you'll learn.'

"He turned the car off, scooped the two hot dog ends into his hand, and got out. He had me put all the tools back in the glove box except for the starting fluid, which he put back under his sweater."

Papa Red paused for a moment and looked over at me. "Don't ask."

He threw up his hands. "That was it! The 'man-work' was over! I felt so good when I walked back into the house. Things were going perfect. I'd gotten a 'man-work' lesson and there weren't no tears, bleeding, or punching involved; it looked like Iron John didn't want nothing else from me; and soon's I walked in the house the smell of spaghetti hitched a ride on the heat and sank into my bones right along with the warmth. Perfect.

"Then Iron John told me, 'Gather them kids up right now.'

"I knew things were going too perfect. I went upstairs, tapped and yelled at the girls' door, 'Iron John wants to see you all.'

"Tee-Tee called out, 'Is supper ready?'

"'Almost, but that's not what he wants; he wants to talk to everybody.'"

"Someone behind the door slammed something on a table and swore.

"I walked over to the boys' room. Little John was in the bottom bunk bed and Herbert was reading a book to him from his bed above.

"'He wants all of us together.'

"Herbert said, 'All of us? What he find out?'

"'I don't know, maybe nothing. He was showing me how to start the Packard.'

"When we got into the hall the girls were waiting for us in front of their door. LaWanda said, 'I don't know which one of y'all did it, but I ain't taking no heat for no one.'

"Herbert said, 'Who asked you to?'

"Once we were in the kitchen Iron John made a show of unbuttoning his coat. I noticed he never pulled the can of starting fluid from under his sweater.

"He said, 'I know how low y'all ungrateful little brats is. I know you be chewing me up in your ungrateful little mouths soon's my back's turned. But I'm here to tell you you ain't got no idea how much I do for y'all, none at all!'

"He pulled out the can of starting fluid. 'Who knows what this is?'

"LaWanda was the only one allowed to talk at these gatherings. She said, 'Isn't that the stuff you spray in the car to get it running?'

"'That's right. And you seen where I was keeping it?'

"'Under your shirt.'

"'And why was it under my shirt? Why would anyone do something that crazy?'

"The answer to that one was pretty simple but none of us was stupid enough to walk into *that* open door.

"LaWanda cut her eyes to the side and said, 'So it would unfreeze and you could spray it in the engine.'

"'And would a bad man do that for his kids? Would someone who's as evil as y'all say I am put a freezing can on his chest so his kids could get in a warm car?'

"Like I said, LaWanda was the only one allowed to talk at these gatherings but we *all* were allowed to keep quiet. And we did.

"'I axed y'all a question. Would a evil man do that for his kids?'

"'No, sir.'

"'So, I guess that proves my point; that proves how wrong y'all is. That proves y'all ain't got no idea how much I sacrifice for you worthless little brats. I'd do anything for y'all, even if it meant hurting myself. Even if it meant I had to damage parts of my own body. Even if it meant doing this. . . .'

"Iron John set the can on the kitchen table, reached his bare hand back under his shirt, and clenched his teeth and his eyes at the same time. He tugged hard at the right side of his chest, let out a little yip of pain then did the same exact thing on the left side of his chest. Keeping his eyes squinched shut, he took a couple of deep breaths like he was trying to get his strength back. Then he brought his balled-up, shaking hand from under his shirt. He opened his eyes and blinked real fast for a few seconds.

"'Would a selfish, stingy man do this for his kids so's they could ride in a warm Packard auto-mobile?'

"He put his still-clinched fist right in front of all of us before he said, 'Would a bum risk this for some trifling, low-life babies?'

"He slowly unclinched his fist and no one even breathed for a good three seconds as we all stared into his palm. There sat two round, reddish brown, raggedy little circles of meat.

"Iron John said, 'Now I'ma have to find me a doctor to sew these back on.'

"One part of my mind knew exactly what these little circle things were but another part of my head was spinning and thinking, 'His nipples! This country fool ripped his nipples off his chest!'

"Iron John dropped them on the table, said, 'One of y'all wrap them up in some wax paper so I can take 'em to the emergency room after I eat,' then walked out of the kitchen.'

"I looked at the little kids and they'd all gone stiff with the same look of shock and horror. Even LaWanda had a minute of doubt. She walked up to the table, looked close, and said, 'No way.'

"Herbert went over to the meat circles next. He picked them up and sniffed.

"Little John yelled, 'No, Herbie! Don't touch them things! Daddy's said he's gonna see a doctor and—'

"Before L.J. could finish Herbert popped the hot dog tips into his mouth. He chewed loud with his mouth wide open then said, 'A little salty but not bad considering they come off such a stinking, nasty old goat.'

"That was too much for the kids. They grabbed each other and screamed out of the kitchen, looking like a four-legged ball of teeth and tears.

"LaWanda told Herbert, 'What do they say? When it comes to being a idiot the apple never falls far from the tree. I don't know which of y'all is the biggest fool.'

"Me and the older kids had figured it out. Sure it took a little longer for some of us to get it than others, but before we left the kitchen that Friday night we knew Iron John and Herbert hadn't done anything more than pull a stunt with some hot dog tips. After a while it even seemed kind of funny.

"Tee-Tee and L.J. all saw it as something a whole lot more serious. And I guess you really can't blame 'em neither."

Papa Red stopped talking again. I thought the story was over. I could see tears in his eyes. But then he said, "I was probably a lot smarter than L.J. and Tee-Tee when I was their age, but it still might've give me a night or two of being scared if I really thought someone was pulling chunks off their body. And I know it would've shook me up even more if I saw my idiot brother, who one time ate a dead, maggoty sparrow on a dare without throwing up, had gone and swallowed someone's nipples before the person could get 'em sewed back on by a doctor."

Papa Red covered his face with his hand and sobbed.

I went to his chair and touched his arm.

He looked at me and said, "They couldn't sleep for months without waking up screaming.

"That last night before he died me and Herbert and LaWanda had laughed about it."

My grandfather cried into his hands again.

Man, why does this stuff always happen to me? I didn't know what to say, so I said what everyone does and sounds so stupid saying, "It's gonna be okay, Papa Red."

He said, "It's kind of funny, we all remembered that night with the hot dogs in different ways. LaWanda called it 'The Night Iron John Lost the Ability Ever to Nurse Anything.' Tee-Tee and L.J. always called it 'That Night When Herbie Ate Daddy's Nibbles.' And Herbert always called it 'The Spaghetti Night That I Got More Meat Than the Rest of You Fools.'"

He cried harder into his hands.

Great. Now I started getting teary. I told Papa Red, "Hold on, Gramps, I'll get us some tissue."

I took a couple of steps toward his door when it felt like a red hot bolt of lightning shot through my shoulder. I didn't know what it was until I heard the "Pie-ow!" sound. I'm a whole lot smarter than Chester: I fought the pain and got out the door. I turned back and looked at Papa Red and his old, shorter switch.

He said, "Don't bother with the tissue. I gotta perfectly good sleeve. What I want you to do is send in that smart-mouth one and don't tell him nothing 'bout this. Me and that boy still got some business to take care of."

He cracked the glowing, humming switch twice more.

I shook my head and walked down the hall. I sure hope this insanity stuff isn't inherited, 'cause it's obvious I come from a whole long line of nutcases.

"Chester? Where you at? Papa Red wants to see you."

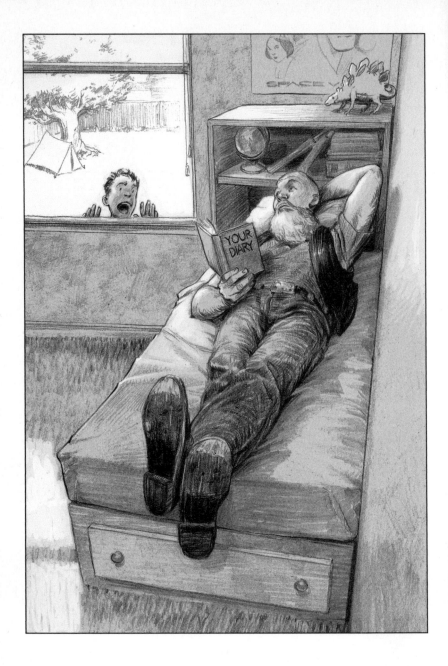

MY PARENTS GIVE MY BEDROOM TO A BIKER

BY PAUL FEIG

This all started because I wouldn't take out the trash.

Now, before you go judging me, I just want to make it clear that I'm not the kind of lazy kid who's bad or hates to be useful around the house. I've helped my mom vacuum and my dad clean out the garage so many times I should get some kind of gold medal from the President of the United States. I've heard them tell our relatives on several occasions that I'm a "good son." I'm the only kid I know who actually *likes* broccoli and eats it at every meal. Even my teachers say I'm pretty polite and responsible and always get my homework in on time. (Well, except for once when our neighbor's dog escaped and attacked me when I was waiting at the bus stop with my science project and since it was a moldy bread experiment, a dog actually *did* eat my homework.)

So, the fact that my parents would get that upset at me about something so stupid and trivial as not taking out the garbage one time only makes them look bad, not me.

Especially when you hear about all the trouble it caused.

This whole insane episode started on this really hot day in July when it was super humid out. You know, that kind of humidity where you come out of your air-conditioned house and before you even close the door behind you, you're sweatier than some guy who just ran across a boiling desert. I had decided to avoid the heat and was comfortably lying on the living room couch watching a supercool show on TV where they blow up stuff to prove scientific theories. So, when my dad told me to take out the garbage as he was leaving to go to work, I just said okay and told myself I'd do it as soon as there was a commercial break.

And then I forgot all about it.

And since my mom didn't hear my dad ask me to take the garbage out and must have assumed he did it himself and since she didn't leave the house all day and didn't see that the cans weren't out front when the garbage truck came by, no one knew there were still three full cans of really smelly garbage sitting in our roasting hot garage until my dad came home and opened the garage door and got a barf-inducing whiff and flipped his lid.

"You never do anything we tell you to do!" he yelled at me after he burst into my room *without knocking* even though for all he knew I could have been in my underwear or had my finger halfway up my nose because I didn't have any warning that someone was going to barge in. "You only think of yourself! You're the most irresponsible, self-centered, lazy kid I've ever met!" And then he slammed the door and stormed off down the hallway.

A bit scared by how angry he had been, I just sat there and waited for him to come back and tell me what my punishment was going to be even though it was totally unfair of him to say such mean things to me. I figured I was probably going to get grounded or have to give up a week's allowance or lose my TV privileges, since that's what happened the other few times I've gotten in trouble. Making things worse, however, was the fact that I had screwed up just the day before when I accidentally broke the window on my mom's china cabinet because I thought it would be a genius idea to try and hit a golf ball with a tennis racket in the living room. My folks were so mad at me about that goof-up that they hadn't even thought of a punishment severe enough to fit my crime yet. And so I had to figure that whatever double sentence was about to be handed down to me was going to be a doozy.

But no punishment came.

The only thing that happened was my mom knocked on my door and told me it was time for dinner. I came out and sat at the table and my mom brought me my side plate of broccoli (that neither of them would touch because they hate broccoli) and we all ate. Neither of them would talk to me and they kept exchanging looks with each other, but no one said anything about me being punished.

And so I did my homework, watched TV for a while, and went to bed.

The next day, I went over to my friend Brian's house and we sat in his basement and played a video football game. For some reason, my brain was working pretty well because I ended up beating Brian three times in a row, which I had never done, since Brian's pretty much the greatest video football player I know. The few times we had played actual football in gym class, Brian had been about the worst player in the history of the world. But when it came to pushing buttons and coming up with strategies for fake guys on the TV screen, Brian was the king.

I was feeling pretty triumphant as I walked home through the humid afternoon air and was even rehearsing an apology to my mom for all the trouble I had caused in the past couple of days, complete with a plan to use some of my secret savings to pay for a new china cabinet window.

So, you can imagine my surprise when I walked through the kitchen and down the hallway and opened the door to my bedroom and found a guy sitting on my bed.

"Who are you?!" I blurted out, practically pooping in my pants from the shock of seeing some strange guy sitting in my room. He looked to be in his thirties and had a scraggly beard and was chewing gum and wearing a black leather motorcycle jacket and big black boots, which were getting mud all over my bedspread.

"Who the crap are *you*?" he said back, not looking up from my expensive, limited-edition Spider-Man comic book that he had taken out of the wrapper and was now getting all creased with his giant dirty hands.

"This is *my* room," I said, both scared of him but also mad that he was making such a mess.

"Not anymore it's not," he said as he flipped a page, then tore off a corner and stuck his gum inside it.

"Hey, that costs a lot of money!" I yelled. "Put it down and get out of my room!"

He lowered the comic book down onto his chest and stared at me like he thought I was the biggest pest he'd ever met in his life.

"Look, kid, are you deaf or something?" he said calmly. "I just told you. This ain't your room no more. Your parents gave it to me. They also said I could have everything in it. So, if you got a problem, why don't you go cryin' to them about it? Meanwhile, quit flappin' your lips and beat it."

He started reading the comic book again, then pulled out a cigarette and lit it.

"Hey, you can't smoke in my room!"

"Already told you once, ain't your room no more," he said again as he flung the smoldering match onto the carpet and blew a ton of smoke toward the ceiling.

Unsure what to do, I ran out of the room to find my mom.

"MOM!" I called. "MUH-THER!"

"Keep your voice down!" I heard her yell from the living room. "You know there's no hollering in the house!"

I ran in and found her sitting on the couch watching TV, drinking a cup of tea like there was nothing at all wrong.

"There's a guy in my bedroom," I said, panicked.

"His name is Carl and it's his room now," she said as she lifted the teacup to her lips and took a sip.

"What do you mean it's his room?"

"Carl is a very nice person and he takes out the garbage and he doesn't break things, and so your father and I decided that he should have your room."

I stared at her in shock.

"What?" was all I could say.

My mom sighed and put her teacup down onto the saucer she was holding. It clinked loudly.

"Carl also listens and hears what we say the first time so we don't have to repeat things constantly, unlike with you, who never seems to listen to a word that comes out of our mouths."

"How could you give away my room?" I asked, feeling like I was losing my mind.

"How *couldn't* we?" she said as her eyes went back to the TV. She then motioned with her head toward something next to the front door. "Your father pulled his old tent out of the attic. You can sleep in the backyard for one week. After that, you need to find somewhere else to live." She then pointed at a garbage bag lying next to the tent. "And take that bag of horrible stuff with you."

"But . . ."

"Don't make me count to five," she said as she glared at me out of the corner of her eye, then over at the broken window in her china cabinet. "You do *not* want to make me count. Trust me."

Completely freaked, I walked over to the front door and grabbed the rolled-up tent and the garbage bag next to it. I looked inside the bag.

It was filled with all the broccoli that had been in our refrigerator.

I stared back at my mom, who was now engrossed in her show, and then went outside.

Boy, she really *was* mad at me.

I set up the tent, which was really small and old and smelled like the inside of somebody's gym shoe. If I thought it was humid outside, being in an old canvas pup tent was like being inside of a boiling teakettle. I dumped all the broccoli in the corner in case I needed something to eat later, crawled out, and went over to my bedroom window. I peered inside and saw that Carl was still sitting on my bed. However, he wasn't reading my comic book anymore. He was now looking through my journal and laughing really loudly.

"Hey!" I yelled, tapping on the window. "That's mine! It's private. Give me that!"

"Sorry." He shrugged. "It's in the room, so it's mine."

He then flipped the page and read some more. "Man," he said, laughing and shaking his head at whatever he just read. "You are such a loser."

Look, since I know what's in my journal, I couldn't argue with him about how embarrassing my personal life was, but that didn't erase the fact that he was reading something of mine that was supposed to be super top secret.

"Give it to me!" I yelled as I pounded on the window with my fist.

"HEY, YOU'D BETTER NOT BREAK THAT GLASS!" my father yelled as he came storming toward me from around the corner of the garage.

"Dad!" I said, happy to see him. "Mom gave away my room to some guy!"

"No, she didn't," he said angrily as he grabbed my arm and pulled me into the yard. "*We* did and his name is Carl, for your information."

"I *know* his name is Carl! I'm *sorry* that I forgot to take out the trash and broke the china cabinet! I'll pay for the window and I'll drive the garbage over to the dump on my bike, I promise. Just let me have my room back!"

"Too little, too late, my friend," my dad said with a snort. "I wish I could say it was nice knowing you. But I don't like to lie."

And with that, my dad walked around the corner and into the house. I looked back at my bedroom window and saw Carl staring at me. Carl then held up my journal, made a super mocking face at me to show what a whiny little girl he thought I was, then laughed and pulled down the shade so I couldn't see in anymore.

In case you couldn't tell, something really weird was going on.

Life got very strange over the next two days.

Through the front window, I could see Mom and Dad sitting around the dining room table with Carl for each meal. He would talk really loudly and act out things like fighting with people and shooting guns and pretending to stab things with a knife, and my parents would laugh and smile at him like he was some kind of hilarious comedian. He even ate with his hands and put his feet up on the table and burped so loudly once it rattled the windows, and yet they just acted like they thought he was the most charming, witty guy they had ever seen in their lives. If I had ever raised my voice or tried to be funny at the dinner table, my mom would yell at me to "settle down," and the one time I accidentally burped because I drank some soda too quickly, you would have thought I had murdered somebody, the way my parents both shouted and carried on about what a pig I was.

On top of all this, that Carl guy looked like he hadn't taken a bath in about a year. Every part of his body was dirty and his hair was greasy and stringy and his beard had food in it from every meal I think he'd ever eaten in his life. He wore the same exact clothes every day, and from the way he'd smelled when I talked to him in my room that first day, I can guarantee he hadn't changed his socks or underwear since socks and underwear were first invented. The guy was pretty much everything my parents used to hate in people, and yet for some reason they seemed to be in love with this guy.

Maybe they had lost their minds. Maybe my parents had always been secretly crazy and it just took me not taking out the garbage to make them snap. Maybe whatever was holding my mom's sanity together came unglued the minute that golf ball went through her china cabinet window. Maybe I really *was* better off being out of the house and out of their lives and moving on to a different life in a different town.

But my parents *weren't* crazy. I'd known them too long to believe that they were. If anything, they were too *normal*. And so them suddenly kicking me out of the house and being all in love with this super scuzzy guy just didn't make sense on any level.

And so for the sake of my parents and for the sake of us as a family, I vowed to figure out just what the heck was going on.

The next morning, I heard a loud engine start up.

I crawled out of my tent and ran around the side of the house just in time to see Carl roar out of the driveway and head off down the street on a huge motorcycle. I then waited until my dad left for work and for my mom to drive off to go shopping. Once she was gone, I got the spare key that we kept hidden in a fake hollow rock under the bush next to our front door and went inside. Everything looked pretty normal except for a lot of scuff marks and mud stains from Carl's boots all over the house. When I looked in the refrigerator, it was filled with beer, which I knew had to be Carl's since neither my mom nor my dad drank alcohol. And when I looked in the bathroom next to my bedroom, I saw the toilet seat was covered with pee, which meant that Carl didn't put it up when he whizzed. The inside of the toilet also was covered with skid marks, which meant that Carl was taking some pretty huge dumps in there and no one was making him clean it up with a toilet brush the way my mom always made me do even if there was the smallest stain in the bowl.

But it wasn't until I walked in my room that I almost fainted.

The place was totally destroyed. There were garbage and pizza boxes and empty beer cans and half-eaten sandwiches lying all over the place. All my sci-fi posters had been torn down, and pictures from biker magazines of women in bikinis were hanging everywhere. All the clothes from my closet had been thrown on the floor, and inside the closet were stacks and stacks of boxes that looked like they had been stolen from some warehouse.

Just as I was about to open one of the boxes, I heard the front door open and Carl yell, "Anybody home?"

Panicked, I tried to run out of the room but heard Carl's big boots clunking down the hallway at top speed. I looked at the window and thought about trying to jump out it, but I knew that my window always stuck and so by the time I got it opened, Carl would already be in the room. And so I crawled under the bed and held my breath, trying not to make a sound.

Carl said, "In here," and then he walked in the room, followed by two other sets of big black, clunky boots.

"Man, this room really *is* the worst," a voice even scarier than Carl's said.

"What nerd used to live in here?" a third even *scarier* voice asked.

"The nerd who's living in a pup tent in the backyard." Carl guffawed as they all laughed with him. "Speaking of nerds, you have *gotta* hear this!"

I heard Carl crack open my journal and clear his throat to start reading.

How embarrassing.

"'Dear Journal,'" Carl read in a super insulting, mocking voice, "'wore my new jeans to school today to impress Sheila Kaufman. When I walked into homeroom, everybody including Sheila stared at me. I was sure they thought I was cool until they all started laughing, and it turned out that my fly was wide open, wide enough for the whole class to see my Superman underwear. I wanted to die.'"

Carl and the other two guys practically fell on the floor in hysterics, and I debated whether I should jump out from under the bed, grab my journal, and make a run for it. But since I was trying to figure out what was wrong with my parents, I decided that I would have to sacrifice my dignity for the time being.

"All right, enough screwing around," Carl finally said. "Let's get to work."

I heard them start tearing open the boxes from the closet

and then heard a bunch of clinking and clanking as they started pulling stuff out. I tried to peek out from under the bed to see what was inside the boxes, but they had their backs to me and so I couldn't tell.

After a few minutes, the scariest voiced guy said, "Where do we keep these?"

"Look and see if there's room under the bed," the second guy said.

Oh no . . .

"Wait, we have to take these to the place," Carl said. "We can't leave anything important in here because pretty soon there's going to be nothing left of this room."

The guys all grunted in agreement and then headed out. I heard them open the front door and slam it shut. I wiggled out from under my bed and ran to the living room window to see what they were carrying, but all I saw was the smoke from their motorcycles as they rounded the corner and roared off toward the main avenue.

I ran back to my room and looked at the now-empty boxes scattered everywhere. Inside them were tons of packing peanuts. I stuck my hand down into them and felt around, but there was nothing left in the boxes. I spun them around to see if they were labeled, but they were all blank. The only thing I really knew was that whatever had been inside those boxes had been metal and that Carl and his friends had taken the items somewhere. I wasn't sure what those things were but I could pretty much guarantee they weren't something good.

"WHAT ARE YOU DOING IN HERE?!"

I almost had a heart attack as I spun around and saw my dad standing in the doorway. His hair was messy and greasy and he hadn't shaved in days.

"You are *not* allowed in this house!" he yelled, his face red with anger. "You *know* that!"

"But Dad," I blurted, "Carl is going to do something terrible to my room. He was just in here with two other guys, and I think they were taking guns or weapons or something out of these boxes."

"You were *spying* on them?!"

Before I could answer, my dad grabbed me by the arm and dragged me through the house. He smelled pretty bad and I realized he'd been wearing the same clothes since the day he gave my room away. He pulled me out the back door, then grabbed my pup tent and yanked it up out of the ground, sending the tent stakes flying. When he did, the broccoli I had inside the tent flew all over the place.

"AAGGH!" he yelled as the broccoli hit him in the face, freaking out like it was a bee trying to sting him. "*Why do you have that?!* Your mother told you to throw it away! WHY DO YOU NEVER LISTEN?!"

Stepping around the pieces of broccoli like they were dog turds, he bunched up the tent into a ball and shoved it into my arms. "Here! Take your tent and your disobedient self and leave our yard. *For good!*"

"But Dad, something weird is going on! I heard Carl say they were going to destroy my room. He and his friends are going to do something bad!"

"Maybe if you spent a little more time trying to fix *yourself* instead of inventing stories about fine, upstanding people, you wouldn't have been kicked out of this house in the first place."

He then dragged me over to the gate, threw it open wide, and pushed me through it into the front yard.

"Do *not* come back, do you hear me?" he said as he glared at me. "Because if you do, I will call the police."

CLINK! My dad slammed the chain-link gate shut and stormed back into the house. Not sure what to do and afraid to upset him even more, I started walking down the driveway toward the street.

As I did, I looked back and saw my mom peeking out at me from behind the living room curtain. She was also wearing the same clothes from days ago and her hair was a mess. The minute we locked eyes, she turned away from the window and pulled the curtain closed.

I looked around the corner of Brian's house at the six motorcycles sitting in our driveway next to my dad's SUV. I had been standing there for hours in the morning heat, waiting to see if Carl and his ever-growing gang were going out on their motorcycles again today. Since my friend Brian and his family were out of town on vacation, I had spent the night in their backyard tree house and decided to use it as my trying-to-find-out-just-what-the-heck-is-going-on headquarters.

Finally, Carl came out of the house with his big scary biker friends. They were carrying huge duffel bags filled with some long things that were clanking loudly as they walked. They got on their motorcycles and fired them up. Just as I was about to jump on Brian's bike that I had taken out of his garage to try and follow them, I saw my mom and dad come out of the house carrying two more duffel bags. Carl waved to them and yelled over his noisy motorcycle, "We'll see you there!"

"We'll be right behind you!" my dad yelled back. "We've just got a couple more bags inside."

As Carl and his gang roared off down the street and around the corner, my parents opened the back of my dad's SUV and put the bags inside. Then they went back into the house. Knowing this was my chance, I ran as fast as I could across the street and jumped into the back of my dad's truck. I pulled open the hatch that the spare tire was hidden in, then yanked out the tire and rolled it into the bushes. I squeezed myself into the small tire space and pulled the hatch down again.

Man, it was a good thing I was a skinny kid who was pretty flexible because it was awfully tight in there.

A few seconds later, something heavy got dropped on top of the hatch door and almost crushed me. It must have been the last of the bags my parents were loading into the truck. Then the truck engine started and I felt the car start to move.

Wherever my parents were going, I was now going with them.

By the time the truck finally stopped a half hour later, I felt like a bug that someone had stepped on. Every bump we'd hit on the road bounced the duffel bags on top of me, and I was pretty sure that if we had driven just a few miles farther I probably would have been flat as a really thin, dead pancake.

The heavy bags were lifted off the hatch as I heard Carl say, "Just put them in the middle of the field." Not being sure where we were or how close anyone was to my dad's truck, I carefully opened the hatch a tiny crack and tried to peek out. All I could see at first was my parents carrying the duffel bags away from the truck. But soon I saw the bikers and my parents placing all the bags in a pile in the middle of a big lawn. I opened the hatch a bit wider and was really surprised at what I saw. . . .

My parents and the bikers were standing at the fifty-yard line in the center of our city's football stadium!

A fat older guy wearing a suit walked up to the bikers. I immediately recognized him from TV as the owner of our city's football team. His suit was pretty rumpled, though, like he had slept in it, and his face was all stubbly from not shaving. He held up a big manila envelope and began to speak.

"All right, everybody, here's how this is going to work. Each of you will take a map and place the canisters from these bags in the specified locations around the stadium. Then tonight, once the crowd is in here for the game, I'll trigger the gas using the master remote as soon as we start the National Anthem. Then, once everybody is unconscious, which will happen quickly because this is very strong stuff, we can get down to business."

The bikers all exchanged excited smiles and laughed like

a bunch of pirates. I couldn't believe my ears. Was this all some big plot to steal things from passed-out football fans? Why would the owner of the football team help them do this? Wasn't he already a rich guy? And most important . . .

I looked at my parents, who looked at the bikers and then started laughing, too.

And then they all high-fived.

What was happening? Were my parents hypnotized? Or were they some kind of criminals who had hidden their true selves from me for all these years but now, in the face of such a big job, had decided they were going to be so rich that they would get rid of me and take their ill-gotten gains and travel the world without the son who broke windows and forgot to take out the garbage?

Whatever the answer was, I knew I couldn't let it happen.

Once my parents had driven the SUV back to our house and gone inside with the bikers, I snuck out of the hatch and tried to find a phone so I could call the police. I went to all our neighbors' houses, but none of them would let me in. They were all really mean to me and wouldn't let me tell them what was wrong and told me to get lost, even though in the past they had all been pretty friendly. But the weird thing was that they were all very dirty and smelly, too, like there had been some order that nobody in town should ever take a shower or wash their clothes again. Even Mrs. Hatfield, the old lady who always baked us cookies and pies, screamed at me to get out of her yard. It was like the whole neighborhood had gone as nuts as my parents.

Realizing I had no other options, I knew I had to ride over to the police station and tell them what was going on. I ran back to Brian's house to get his bike. Since the police station was a few miles away and since I was starving, I went into my tent and grabbed the last pieces of broccoli that were still in there. They were pretty wilted and soft and kind of gross and I had to eat them raw, but when you're trying to stop a major crime from being committed without getting a hunger headache, then beggars can't be choosers.

I jumped on Brian's bike and pedaled quickly across his front yard toward the road. Just as I started to head down the street, I heard footsteps behind me. I looked over my shoulder.

The bikers were running after me as fast as they could! And, man, they were fast.

I tried to speed up, but their hands grabbed me from behind and yanked me off the bike, which rolled down the street, then wiped out and tumbled onto its side, its handlebars now bent.

Oh, man, Brian's gonna kill me if I live through this.

"And where do you think *you're* going?" Carl said as he tossed me over his shoulder while his biker buddies all laughed evilly.

Inside our house, the bikers had tied me to a kitchen chair. My mom and dad were staring at me from across the room, looking very upset. I had been so stunned from getting captured I couldn't speak. Everything was all just too weird.

"The neighbors said you were trying to call the police," my dad finally said. "Any reason why you'd be doing this?"

The bikers stared at me as Carl bent down and put his face right in front of mine. Man, did his beard smell terrible.

"You wouldn't happen to know anything you shouldn't know, would you?" he said threateningly. "You haven't been snooping around and saw or heard something that's none of your business, have you?"

His breath stank so bad that I didn't even want to open my mouth or inhale to talk, so I just sat there and stared back at him as I held my breath.

"If you had just stayed in the backyard like we told you to and not come out of your tent, you wouldn't be in so much trouble," my mom said as she stepped forward. She looked terrible. "But, as always, you just don't listen."

"You gotta tell us what you know, kid," Carl said, his nose practically touching mine. "You'd better open that mouth and start talking or I'll reach down your throat and pull the words right out of you."

I kept holding my breath, but now I was starting to feel like I was going to pass out. Like it or not, I was going to have to breathe in a big whiff of Carl to get some air so I could tell him to get away from me.

PAAAAAAAAHHHHH! I exhaled a huge breath right into his face.

His eyes went wide and he jumped back suddenly, swatting at the air in front of his mouth and nose.

"AAAAHHH!" Carl yelled. "He's been eating broccoli! Get him out of here!"

The other bikers sniffed the air, and then they started freaking out, too, waving their hands around and holding their heads.

"*Broccoli!*" they screamed as they ran out of the room. "NOOOOO!"

My mom and dad sniffed the air and started to panic, too.

"You didn't throw away that broccoli, did you?!" my mother yelled as she started to cry. "You ate it, didn't you? YOU NEVER DO ANYTHING WE TELL YOU—"

BOOM!!!

There was a huge explosion inside the house as all the dishes and pots and pans fell off our kitchen shelves and smashed onto the floor and a cloud of dust blasted in from the hallway.

"IT'S HAPPENING!" my father hollered, and then pointed at me. "GET HIM OUT OF HERE NOW!"

Carl started to move toward me. Freaking out, I exhaled again. Carl and my parents recoiled in fear.

"He's filled with too much broccoli!" Carl yelled. "Just get away from him!"

And then they all ran out of the house.

The ground started shaking like a volcano was erupting. Everything that wasn't nailed down started to fall. Dust and debris continued to blow through the hallway as I heard a loud, hollow sound coming from my bedroom. I had no idea what it was but felt like I had to see what had become of my room and all my stuff. Since my arms were still tied to the chair, I had to bend over and try to walk with the chair tied behind my back.

The wind in the hallway was like a hurricane. I struggled to move forward as all my possessions blew out of my room and hit me in the face. The hollow noise got louder, and the air blowing out of my room started to get hot as I pushed my way through the door.

And that was when I saw the hole.

There, in the middle of my bedroom floor, where my bed used to be, was a huge round opening that went deep into the ground. It was about six feet across and had metal walls. It looked like it went way down, as if it were some sort of futuristic sewer pipe that tunneled straight into the center of the earth. I could hear a low moaning sound deep inside it, and I tried to get to the edge of the hole so I could peek in at what was inside.

WHOOSH!

Suddenly a huge swarm of what looked like ghosts came bursting up out of the hole, knocking me off my feet and sending me flying backward into my desk.

SMASH!

Wood and plaster exploded everywhere. I looked up and saw thousands of the ghosts flying through the ceiling and into the sky. When I looked back down at the hole they were pouring out of, one of the ghosts flew straight at my face, and before I could even move, he went up my nose. And then . . .

I was a different person.

I mean, I knew I was still myself in my body, but that part of me couldn't do anything. My brain had different thoughts, and my body started to move even though I wasn't controlling it. The person inside me held my hands up in front of my eyes and thought, *Finally, I have hands!*

And all of a sudden I knew exactly what was going on.

I was part of an alien race whose home planet is light-years away, but I had been in a giant metal "seed" filled with millions of alien spirits that was sent out thousands of light-years ago and had crashed into the earth a few hundred years ago and had been sitting underground waiting until now to come up through the tube that had always been directly under this bedroom, and all my alien friends and I, who were made of gas and who needed bodies to inhabit so we could take over this planet, were on our way to some giant stadium, where we were all going to get people to live inside, thanks to our leaders, who had taken over some bikers and the parents of the kid I was inside now, and we were going to enslave the rest of the human race and use them to do our dirty work, and *oh no, this body is full of sulforaphane because the kid who owns it has been eating broccoli and I HAVE TO GET OUT OF IT NOW!*

I fell back onto the floor as the alien spirit jumped out of me and flew around in circles like he was having a melt-down before crashing into the wall and knocking himself unconscious.

I looked at him lying on the floor, and now that I was

241

myself again, I realized it was up to me to save the world because I knew exactly how.

And so I did.

It took a lot of convincing on my part to get the army to believe me, but since weird things had been going on in other parts of our country and around the world, they knew that something strange was up. So they eventually decided to give my advice a try. The army all ate tons of broccoli to safeguard themselves against being taken over by aliens, and then they went out with giant semis loaded with broccoli and tons of tanker trucks filled with broccoli juice and made everybody eat broccoli and captured anyone who was acting weird and forced them to drink broccoli juice. And just like that, the alien spirits started jumping out of people and flying back into their underground seed through the hole in my room. Eventually everybody in the world had eaten broccoli, and they were all much healthier on top of not being possessed by aliens anymore. The army then sealed the seed and dug it up and shot it deep into outer space and the world was saved and I was a big hero.

And back at our house, which the army rebuilt for us since it had gotten pretty much destroyed by all of this alien stuff, my parents and Carl and his biker friends sat around having a celebratory dinner where they all thanked me for saving their lives. It turned out that Carl wasn't such a bad guy after all. The alien inside him was much meaner than Carl really was, and although he still wasn't that into hygiene, he wasn't nearly as dirty and stinky as he had been when he was possessed. It turned out that the aliens had no idea how to take care of a human body and didn't have a clue that you needed to wash them and change their clothes every day.

"Here's to our hero," said Carl as he raised his beer in the air, and everyone else raised their glasses and toasted to me.

"You're the best son a parent could ever have," my mom said as she kissed me on the cheek.

"I second that," said my dad as he smiled at me and gave me a wink.

"Thanks," I said back to them all. "And I promise I'll never forget to take out the trash again."

They all laughed, and then Carl leaned back in his chair, burped, and put his feet up.

"Get your feet off the table, Carl," my mom said.

"Yes, ma'am," said Carl.

It was nice to have everything back to normal.

THE BLOODY SOUVENIR
BY JACK GANTOS

My mother was right. I was not my own man. I was a "spineless follower" just as she had always said. I was a boy who was easily led astray. I liked hanging around with dangerous kids who were full of insanely feral ideas that ended in disaster, and I felt lucky that we had recently moved next door to the two most dangerous guys in the world, the Pagoda brothers. Frankie was a skinny, innocent-looking kid who was my age, even though he was covered with about a hundred years' worth of bruises. We were in the same sixth-grade class, though I didn't see him much because he mostly only showed up for lunch and to take his afternoon nap in the puke-smelling nurse's office. Gary Pagoda was in eighth grade, but I was never sure of his age. Maybe he was fifteen or eighteen or even twenty. It was impossible to tell. He had a lot of scar tissue on his face. When I looked at his mouth full of chipped teeth, I thought he might even be twenty-five. But when you considered how he behaved, he might just have been a supersized six-year-old psychopath. One thing I did know is that he had already been to prison. The other thing I knew was that I was vastly jealous that I hadn't been to prison, too, because that is where he got most of his manly facial wounds and body tattoos, which my mother said were "too rude for the naked eye."

Well, you can imagine that my mom did not want me to play with those kind of boys. In fact, she "forbid" me to play with them, especially after Gary had poured a bucket of boat fuel on top of their swimming pool and set it on fire. He made Frankie and me dive in and play like we were the survivors on a Nazi submarine that had been hit with a depth charge. He stood on the end of the diving board and threw cherry bombs into the water as we swam around under the flames. No one was seriously hurt, though Frankie temporarily lost his hearing and I only suffered a little burn from where I popped up for air and set the top of my head on fire. It was no big deal that I had a patch of hair that looked like the remains of a tiny forest fire and smelled like burned rubber. I could tell Mom was annoyed, but she was still at the point where she was hoping I would grow out of this self-destructive stage. It wasn't until a week later when she entered my bedroom and caught me stitching up a three-inch gash over my knee that she lost her temper. I was using one of her sewing needles and some nylon fishing line I had found in the garage.

"You are becoming just like those Pagoda boys," she said harshly.

"No, I'm not," I replied. "I'm smart enough to know the difference between dangerous play and fun play."

"No, you are not," she shot right back. "You are lying to yourself. Mark my words, you'll do something so stupid someday that even you won't be able to deny just how *Pagoda-stupid* you've become."

She was right, of course, I had already become a hazard to myself, but I actually thought I could stop going over there whenever I wanted. *I'm not addicted to stupidity like they are*, I had said to myself. I figured I could just snap my fingers and become a whole different kind of kid—like a choirboy, or a chess genius, or a Latin scholar, but I was wrong. I could snap my fingers until the skin peeled off and I wore the raw flesh down to the bone and I wouldn't change one little bit. In fact, I was even *more* stupid than they were, though I didn't know that just yet.

I thought I was just flirting with danger like when we made the Roman catapult out of a springy pine tree and shot each other across the front yard. I only dislocated my shoulder when I landed on a concrete yard gnome, but Mom didn't find out because Gary popped the joint of my arm back into the socket for me. But this game didn't mean I had totally lost my sense of good judgment. We were only having fun like the time we put on roller skates and blasted down their metal sliding board and through a flaming Hula-hoop at the bottom as their cousin Jennifer Pagoda filmed us. Sure, that was dangerous, but I wasn't compelled to do it like my mom suggested. I did it only after I weighed the consequences and decided it was mostly a safe activity. I had self-control when I wanted to use it. I just didn't want to use it all the time. To me, this was the difference between me and the Pagoda boys. They were obsessed with danger and driven like mindless beasts to hurt themselves. On the other hand, I was just a casual thrill seeker who could give up danger whenever I felt like it.

Or maybe not.

And this is really where my story begins, and where I proved to my mother that I was a pathetic example of a defective human a full rung below *Pagoda-stupid*. I started out the day by exercising some better judgment over at the

Pagoda house. Gary wanted to have a cigarette-smoking contest to see who could suck through a pack the fastest, and I stood up and said, "No way am I doing that!"

"Why not?" Gary asked, and took a quick step toward me as he reached for his knife, which was tucked into his back pocket.

"Because smoking will kill you," I smugly replied. "Ask anyone."

"What if I kill you first?" he suggested, and opened his knife, which was as sharp as a razor. "What is worse? A knife through the neck or a pack of smokes? Answer me that, *brain-boy*."

"I'd rather die with a knife blade through my lungs than smoke a pack of cigarettes and die like a coughing dog," I replied. "Smoking is about the most stupid thing a person can do."

Gary spit tobacco juice on the ground. "Oh, go be a public service announcement and leave us alone," he said, and waved his knife toward my house. "Beat it."

"No problem," I replied, and marched off feeling very proud of myself. I was walking across my front yard while thinking that it was a shame I couldn't tell my mother how mature I had just been because she had forbidden me to play with them in the first place.

I didn't have shoes on because it was hot and shoes made my feet sweat. I took a step and suddenly I got a sharp pain right in the bottom of my left foot. "Ouch!" I yelped. It really hurt. I figured I had stepped on a sharp rock or a piece of glass or a nail. I lifted my foot to see what it was, but it wasn't any of those things. It was a great big wart on the bottom of my foot and it was madly throbbing. How could it have so suddenly grown on me? *Maybe warts are like volcanoes*, I thought, *and they just spring up overnight.* I reached down and touched the painful tip of it. "That is the most disgusting thing I have ever seen," I said out loud as I balanced on my other foot. I figured I had better go in the house and tell Mom, but then I thought, *No, don't tell her. She'll just take you to the doctor, and he'll remove it somehow and that will hurt.* So I concluded that I would take care of this little wart problem myself.

I limped into the house remembering how Gary had showed me two little scars on his hands. When he was born, he had six fingers on each hand but the sixth one, he said, was like a rubber worm. It just limply hung down by the base of his good little finger. There was no bone in it and no way to control it, so it was always getting caught in car doors and dresser drawers, and when he wiped his butt, it always dipped into the toilet water, which was really gross.

So one day when he was ten, he took a pair of garden shears and snipped them off. "Sure it bled a little bit," he said. "But I rubbed dirt on the cut parts and the blood stopped and a week later the skin healed over. It was no big deal."

"What'd you do with the fingers?" I asked.

He grinned sheepishly and leaned toward my ear. "Fishing bait," he whispered. "A little finger food."

"Did you catch anything?" I asked.

"A catfish that was big enough to feed the whole family," he replied. "It was a monster."

So if Gary could snip off his extra fingers, I could just pull my ugly wart out as if it were a bad tooth. How hard could it be?

I opened the front door of the house and didn't see my mom, so I quickly limped down the hallway and slipped into my room. I kept my toolbox on my dresser, and I opened it up and removed a rusty pair of needle-nose pliers I had found in the street. They must have fallen out of the back of a telephone repairman's truck. They were a little dirty-looking, so I rubbed them back and forth on my pants. Then I stood next to my bed with the bottom of my back left foot facing up. I twisted around behind me and with the pliers got a deep, unyielding grip on the wart, and just like my dentist I shouted out, "One, two, three—shazam!" And with all my might I ripped the wart out of the bottom of my foot. Instantly I knew this was not a good idea because I actually heard the sound of ripping flesh, which was like a little zipper sound. And then the blood came squirting right out of that hole in my foot and shot about six feet across the room and hit the wall.

"Arrrgh!" I cried out, and dropped straight to the floor. The pain was crippling. I kept slapping the floor and muttering the magic words against pain, "Mind over matter . . . mind over matter . . . I don't feel a thing!" But the magic words did not work. The pain was massive. I looked back at my foot and a little fountain of blood was spurting out with every beat of my heart. *I'm dying,* I thought. *I've really done it this time.*

After some deep breaths I pulled myself together for a moment and steadied myself against the doorjamb. I peeked around the corner. I didn't see my mom, so I desperately hopped on one foot down the hall toward the bathroom. I glanced over my shoulder and saw little pools of blood scattered behind me. I knew they might lead to trouble with my mom, but there was nothing I could do at the moment but concentrate all my "mind-over-matter" techniques to block out the pain. I kept hopping and zigzagging down the hall like a wounded rabbit until I lunged into the bathroom, spun around, and wisely locked the door behind me.

I was out of breath, and between gasps of air I kept chanting, "Now you have done something really, really stupid!" The blood was still burbling out of my foot when I worked my way over to the tub spigot and turned it on. I knew I should clean the wound, but when the water went into the ragged, bloody hole in my foot, I thought I had been jabbed with a hot poker. "Oh, cheese!" I shouted.

I was blinded by the pain as I danced up and down while splashing bloody water all over the walls. And then just what I dreaded most in the world happened next. There was a loud knocking on the door.

"Jack!" my mother said sharply. "What is going on in there?"

I quickly bit down on my lip and composed myself. "Nothing," I said blithely as if I really were telling the truth.

"Well," she continued, "then can you explain why there are blood drops leading from your bedroom to the bathroom?"

"Oh, I just had a tiny accident," I replied with a jolly chuckle. "No big deal."

"Are you okay?" she pressed.

"Yes," I said in a fake cheerful voice because I was about

to explode. My muscles were so contorted I thought all the bones in my body would snap. "I'll be okay."

"Just make sure you clean up the hall," she ordered, and I heard her turn and walk away.

I instantly shoved a wet washcloth in my mouth and tried not to scream too loudly when suddenly there was more loud knocking on the bathroom door.

"What?" I shouted.

"You didn't do something *stupid* with the Pagoda boys?" she asked, and I could tell by her harsh voice that she was already convinced that I had.

"No!" I shouted back.

"Well, you know you are capable of hurting yourself," she reminded me. "You've done it before."

"I know," I replied indignantly, "but I'm fine."

"Just checking," she added.

"Thank you for your consideration," I said sweetly, "but you may go now." Honestly, I was in so much pain I was ready to beat myself unconscious on the dull edge of the sink.

And she did go! I pressed my ear to the door and heard her walk away, and when I could no longer hear her, I said to myself, "Oh, boy, this time you really did something stupid."

I didn't know what to do next so I opened the medicine chest and looked inside. There was a little plastic bag of cotton balls. I never in my life had noticed them before when suddenly I got one of those "Eureka!" moments.

"They are for stuffing holes!" I shouted joyously. I shook a few from the bag, took a deep breath, and pressed one up into the hole. Then I did another, and another, until the hole was filled up. I stood and pressed my foot down on the floor. It hurt, but I was relieved that the blood had clotted and stopped. Then just to give the cotton balls a little more strength, I took white first aid tape and wrapped it around my foot. *Perfect!* I thought. *It's as good as new.*

I took a towel and wiped up the bloody mess in the bathroom, then crawled down the hall, wiping up the blood drops on the floor until I got into my bedroom.

And there it was—the reward for all that pain. I grinned like an idiot as I knelt down over the puddle of blood. Right in the middle was the rusty pair of pliers, and right at the tip of the pliers was that big hunk of bloody, yellow, warty flesh. I plucked it out and made it over to my bedside table, where I snatched up my journal and then got a knife out of my toolbox. I gouged a hole in the cover of the journal and shoved the juicy wart inside. "That's a keeper," I said, admiring my souvenir of pain as I shuffled over to the window, where I set the journal on the sill to dry under the sun.

That night I slept well, and the next morning I hopped out of bed, but when my foot hit the floor, the pain made me wince and I jerked my foot up. "That's sore," I said, and then added, "Of course it is sore, you idiot. You just ripped a wart out with a pair of pliers. Now suck it up and go to school."

I got dressed, put on some well-padded sneakers, and left the house. For once Frankie Pagoda showed up to school before lunch. He was in my math class.

"Hey," he said, and pointed at my shoe, "how come you are limping?"

With great pride I told him about my self-surgery. He didn't seem terribly impressed. "I'm sure that hurt," he said, "but Gary just burns his warts out with the tip of a soldering iron. When you burn them out, it seals the wound so you don't bleed plus it kills all the germs that could infect you."

"Wow," I said sarcastically, "I didn't know Gary was such a deep thinker."

"He thinks about pain all the time," Frankie said. "Believe me."

I believed him.

The rest of the day was okay. I told the gym teacher I had stepped on a nail, so I got a pass to sit in the library.

The next morning when I rolled out of bed and put my foot on the floor, it seemed extra tender and puffy. And then with some alarm I noticed a red streak was now running out from underneath the bandages. *That can't be good*, I quietly thought as I shrugged it off. *So I'll ignore it.* But all day at school it would not be ignored. It burned. It simmered. It pounded. No matter which way I moved my foot it throbbed as if beating inside the wound was a tiny, angry heart. I started to worry but then I got a grip on myself. "Suck it up!" I hissed. "A wound always gets worse before it gets better." I didn't know if that was true but Gary had said it was.

The following day I got out of bed and my foot was like a hot anvil and the red streak was above my ankle and heading for my knee. I took a deep breath. "I'll just pretend I didn't see that," I said bravely, and limped off to school, where all day I could think of nothing but my screaming foot.

The next morning was worse. When I stood up my foot was killing me, and then I looked into the mirror and saw I was covered with hundreds of pussy little pink boils all over my body. "Oh, creeping crud," I moaned. "I'm dying!" In a panic I hopped out of the room and careened off the walls all the way down to the kitchen, where my mother was making coffee.

"Look at me!" I shouted hysterically, and held open my PJ top so she could see the boils. "I'm dying!"

"Mother of mercy!" she shouted in return, and stepped back in horror. "You are dying! Now get some clothes on and get in the car."

I chicken-hopped back up to my room and pulled on some clothes and my sneakers and met her at the car. She looked insane, so I thought I must be dying, and when she hit the gas, we flew out of the driveway and down the street. Gary Pagoda was standing on the corner. It was hard to tell if he was just coming home from a wild night out or if he was going to school because he had the kind of hair that was always damp-looking, so you couldn't tell if he had just taken a morning shower or if he had a sweaty head from running from the police. As we passed him, I saw that he was holding a baby alligator between his thumb and forefinger.

I waved to him.

"Don't wave to him!" Mom ordered. "You'll only encourage his sick behavior."

I lowered my hand to my lap. As I did so, I saw the boils

along my arms and closed my eyes. It scared me to look at myself.

It didn't take long for Mom to pull up to the hospital emergency entrance. "I'm warning you," she said as she stomped on the brakes and threw the gear shift into Park. "You'd better tell the truth or I'll kill you, because I'm sure you did something stupid."

"You are scaring me," I said weakly. "Please don't."

"I'm your mother," she replied. "I'm supposed to scare you, so don't tell me how to behave. Now get a move on."

Inside the emergency room we were directed into a small alcove that was sealed off by a white curtain. I sat on a bench and my mother sat next to me.

"What stupid thing have you done?" she whispered, with her fist hovering over her shoulder. "Tell me before the doctor gets here so you don't embarrass me."

Just at that moment the doctor pulled aside the curtain. "Well," he said, after taking a long look at me, "what do we have here?" He sat on a stool, and with the rubber tip of his pencil he began to poke my boils. He took my temperature and then looked inside my mouth.

"I think he has done something stupid," my mom blurted out. "He does stupid stuff all day long."

"Is there something unusual you have done to yourself?"

the doctor asked calmly, trying to offset my mother's tone. "You can tell me. I won't think it's stupid."

"Well . . ." I said, getting ready to tell him, when I made a mistake and glanced at my mom. That big fist of hers was still making a circle above her shoulder, and she was squinting at me like she wanted to split my skull. One wrong word and I knew she would knock me to the other side of the room.

I turned back to the doctor. "No," I said innocently. "I can't think of anything unusual I may have done. This is a complete mystery to me."

"Peculiar," he replied. "I think you should go into the next room." And he pointed toward another curtained space. I stood up and half smiled at my mom. She nicked her chin with her fist as a warning while she mouthed, *"Tell the truth or else!"*

I was so happy to get away from her that for a moment I forgot I was dying. But it didn't take long before I remembered. In an instant a big nurse in a stiff white dress pulled aside the curtain and looked at me revoltingly as if I were infected with the plague.

"Take off all your clothes and stand like an X in the middle of the room," she ordered.

"Did I hear you correctly?" I asked.

"Like a big naked X!" she snapped. "Now, no monkey business." Then she pulled the curtain closed and dashed off.

I did what I was told, taking off all my clothes, and that's when I saw the bandages—no way was the nurse not going to notice those. I peeled them off, slowly, throwing them in the garbage by the curtain. My foot looked like the big hunk of ham you see behind the counter at the deli. Blood immediately started seeping through the cotton balls, but I pressed my foot against the ground to keep it all in. If I angled my foot in a bit, you couldn't even see the red streak, which was almost at my knee, unless you were looking directly at it.

Before she returned I got into my big naked X position. I looked straight up at the blinding lightbulb because I couldn't bear to stare down at my naked, pus-covered self. In a moment the nurse returned. In one hand she had something like a gallon of paint in a bucket and in the other she had a wide paintbrush. She surveyed me up and down with her eyes. I dropped my hands to cover my private parts.

"Don't you dare touch yourself!" she snapped. "Now get those hands in the air, mister!"

I threw my hands straight up as if she had pulled a gun on me.

"Now stand still while I paint you with this medicine," she growled, "or I'll put you in quarantine with the rabid animals."

I stiffened up as she dipped the brush into the bucket and began to paint me from the top of my head on down, and to my dismay the medicine was bright, neon purple.

"What is this?" I whimpered.

"An antifungal agent," she replied as she brushed my chest up and down like a fence. "It's called Gentians Violet, and we paint kids with it who have really bad hygiene. Now stick out your hand."

I did as I was told and she pressed the brush handle into my palm. "Now swab your private parts—both front and back and all around your behind," she instructed. "Do a good job because the parts and cracks of the body that don't get much sunlight are where fungus hides and grows."

I didn't need to know that.

She watched with her big hands on her hips as I did a very thorough job, and while I had the brush, I ran it down the red streak on my leg and over my foot. Then I gave her back the brush. It didn't take long before she was finished and I was glowing purple from head to toe. I stood still for as long as it took to dry off then put my clothes on and slowly ambled out to my mother. She looked at me and grimaced. "You look like a pickled beet," she said, shaking her head in amazement.

"Can I have a hug?" I asked, and held my arms open.

"Maybe tomorrow," she replied, poking at my skin. "You are still tacky."

Thankfully, we were both quiet on the ride home, but when we pulled back into the driveway, my sister was just leaving the house. "Oh, puke!" she shouted as I stepped from the car and into the full sunlight. I was blinding to look at, and she covered her eyes with one hand as she shouted out loud to the neighborhood, "Hey, everyone, come see our new yard gnome. Its name is Purple Pus Boy!"

I lowered my head and marched toward the front door. "Thanks for all your kindness," I hissed as I passed her. I went into my room and closed the bedroom door. I took off my shoe and then peeled off my sock, which was already soaking through with blood, and wrapped bandages around it again. The clean wrapping felt better but not by much. Then I got up and walked over to the windowsill, where my journal was drying out. I reached forward and touched the pebbly surface of the wart. It was great, and I smiled just a little.

That night my mother brought me my dinner on a tray.

"I thought you'd rather avoid the family spotlight," she said, and reached out to hug me but then remembered that I was repulsive and pulled away ·with a look of fear and loathing.

The next morning I woke up and when I put my foot down on the floor, I knew there was a problem. It felt like that little volcanic wart had erupted and now I was standing on red-hot molten lava. And then there was the streak. Even though I was purple, I could still see it. I almost wanted to cry because now it was running up the inside of my leg, over my hip, and aiming for my heart. "This can't be good," I said slowly, and instantly I knew the terrible, hard thing that I was going to have to do. I put on a pair of long pants and a long-sleeved shirt, and pulled a baseball cap down low over my forehead, and slipped my hands into a pair of work gloves, and painfully limped down the hall.

"Hey, Mom," I said as casually as I knew how. "I forgot to tell the doctor one little bitsy thing that I think would be really helpful for my future health."

She gave me a withering look that would scare a bear. "Back in the car," she commanded with one stiff finger pointing toward the front door.

I got into the car as if I were taking a ride to where I

would meet a firing squad. The whole way there she drove with one hand on the wheel and the other balled up into a red fist and aimed at me. She knew I had done something colossally stupid. But I still wouldn't tell her what. And why should I? She'd never understand. It was a boy thing.

She pulled into the parking lot. "Out!" was all she said.

I scurried from the car and hobbled up the stairs and into the emergency room. Very sick people pulled back from me. The ones who were too sick to move just closed their eyes.

The nurse receptionist escorted us to the same little room with the curtain. My mom and I sat on the same bench. She held the same fist up in the air, but she looked at me in a new way, a way that confirmed all her fears. "You are one of them," she said, passing a final judgment on me. "You've become a Pagoda. Admit it!"

Before I could put together some flimsy lie, the doctor pulled aside the curtain and stepped toward me. "What did you forget to tell me?" he asked.

"Yes," my mother echoed, "what did you *forget* to tell us?"

There was no other way to say it except to blurt it out. "It slipped my mind the other day," I said breathlessly, and I pointed toward my foot. "I had this big volcanic wart on the bottom of my foot, and I took this rusty pair of needle-nose pliers, and . . . and . . . and ripped it out!"

"Ripped it out?" my mother shrieked. "Are you kidding me! Ripped it out with a pair of pliers! Oh save me, doctor," she said mournfully, "my son is an idiot."

The doctor patted her on the knee to calm her down as he looked up at me. "You know what you did, don't you?"

"No," I replied, "I'm too stupid to know what I did. What'd I do?"

"You gave yourself blood poisoning with the rusty pair of pliers," he explained.

"Oh," I said quietly as my pride shriveled up like the ugly wart in my journal.

Then the doctor gently removed the bandages and looked at what I did. Neither he nor my mother said anything. They just sadly shook their heads, which was worse, in a way. The doctor gave me antibiotics.

On the way home I tried to tell my mother I would never do something this stupid again. "I promise," I said tearfully. I raised my hand and began to cross my heart to swear on it, but she reached out and clamped down on my hand with a steel grip.

"Don't cross your heart and hope to die," she warned me, "because you will. Even if I cut your legs off, you will drag your severed torso across the ground to go over to that

Pagoda madhouse and somehow maim yourself."

She was right. I would. I knew I'd take the antibiotics and get over my boils, but when it came to the Pagodas, I was infected for life and there was no cure from them other than death. Or maybe if I was extremely lucky, I would only be crippled for life.

"Mom," I asked, and reached for her free hand. I lifted it up to my purple lips and kissed it. "If I were paralyzed and strapped to a bed, and in a coma, and unable to speak, would you take care of me?"

"Of course," she said without hesitation. "I'm your mother. I'm compelled to take care of you even if you can't take care of yourself."

Yessss! I thought. Just then we turned the corner on to our street and Gary Pagoda was on the peak of his roof, balanced precariously on a unicycle.

This is going to be good, I thought. I turned and looked at my mother. She was staring up at Gary and then she winced. I turned back to watch Gary, but he was gone and all I heard was a bloodcurdling scream. A little later we heard the ambulance. And that night Mom was in such a great mood, she baked her special-occasion red velvet cake with chocolate icing. And I got busy writing Gary a get-well-soon card. I was sure his spine would heal just fine and he'd return to us soon. I'd be waiting for him. Now that I had one souvenir in my journal, I was ready for another. Perhaps a tooth, or a toe tip, or a bit of earlobe—something that my mother would never understand.

ABOUT GUYS READ

Guys Read funny stuff. And you just proved it. (Unless you just opened the book to this page and started reading. In which case, I feel bad for you because you've missed some pretty funny stuff.)

Now what?

Now we keep going—Guys Read keeps working to find good stuff to read, you read it and pass it along to other guys. Here's how we can do it.

For ten years, Guys Read has been at www.guysread.com, collecting recommendations of what guys really want to read. We have gathered thousands of great funny books, scary books, action books, illustrated books, information books, wordless books, sci-fi books, mystery books, and you-name-it books.

So what's your part of the job? Simple: you read more, try out some of the suggestions at guysread.com, try some of the other stuff written by the authors in this book, then let us know what you think. Tell us what you like to read. Tell us what you don't like to read. The more you tell us, the more great book recommendations we can collect. It might even help us choose the writers for the next installment of Guys Read.

You've read the *Funny Business*. Prepare yourself for Mystery/Thrillers, Action/Adventure, Real Stuff, and more.

Thanks for reading.

And thanks for helping Guys Read.

JON SCIESZKA (editor and coauthor, "Your Question for Author Here") has been writing books for children ever since he took time off from his career as an elementary school teacher. He wanted to create funny books that kids would want to read. Once he got going, he never stopped. He is the author of numerous picture books, middle grade series, and even a memoir. From 2007–2010 he served as the first National Ambassador for Children's Literature, appointed by the Library of Congress. Since 2004, Jon has been actively promoting his interest in getting boys to read through his Guys Read initiative and website. Born in Flint, Michigan, Jon now lives in Brooklyn with his family. Visit him online at www.jsworldwide.com.

SELECTED TITLES

THE TRUE STORY OF THE THREE LITTLE PIGS
(Illustrated by Lane Smith)

THE STINKY CHEESE MAN AND
OTHER FAIRLY STUPID FAIRY TALES
(Illustrated by Lane Smith)

The Time Warp Trio series
(Illustrated by Lane Smith)

KNUCKLEHEAD: *Tall Tales & Mostly True Stories
of Growing Up Scieszka*

ROBOT ZOT (Illustrated by David Shannon)

MAC BARNETT ("Best of Friends") is the author of three picture books and a middle grade series called the Brixton Brothers, the first installment of which was nominated for an Edgar Allen Poe Award. He serves on the board of directors of 826LA, a nonprofit writing/tutoring center fronted by a convenience store for time travelers, the Echo Park Time Travel Mart (motto: Whenever You Are, We're Already Then). Visit him at www.macbarnett.com.

SELECTED TITLES

BILLY TWITTERS AND HIS BLUE WHALE PROBLEM
(Illustrated by Adam Rex)

GUESS AGAIN!
(Illustrated by Adam Rex)

OH NO!
(Illustrated by Dan Santat)

THE BRIXTON BROTHERS: THE CASE OF THE CASE
OF MISTAKEN IDENTITY
(Illustrated by Adam Rex)

EOIN COLFER ("Artemis Begins") is the author of the phenomenally successful Artemis Fowl series, as well as many other books for kids. Before he started writing, he was an elementary school teacher. He knew he wanted to write from a young age, however—ever since he first started reading Viking stories in school. His first name, in case you were wondering, is pronounced "Owen." He lives in Ireland. You can visit him at www.eoincolfer.com.

CHRISTOPHER PAUL CURTIS ("'What? You Think *You* Got It Rough?'") is the author of BUD, NOT BUDDY, which won the Newbery and Coretta Scott King Medals, and THE WATSONS GO TO BIRMINGHAM—1963, which received Newbery and Coretta Scott King Honors. He is also the author of ELIJAH OF BUXTON, which won the Scott O'Dell Historical Fiction Award in addition to Newbery and Coretta Scott King Honors. He was born in Flint, Michigan, and now lives with his family in Ontario, Canada.

KATE DiCAMILLO (coauthor, "Your Question for Author Here") won the Newbery Medal for her book THE TALE OF DESPEREAUX. Her other books include BECAUSE OF WINN-DIXIE, which received a Newbery Honor, and THE TIGER RISING, which was a National Book Award finalist. She lives in Minneapolis, Minnesota. You can find her online at www.katedicamillo.com.

SELECTED TITLES

BECAUSE OF WINN-DIXIE

THE TALE OF DESPEREAUX

THE TIGER RISING

THE MIRACULOUS JOURNEY OF EDWARD TULANE
(Illustrated by Bagram Ibatoulline)

THE MAGICIAN'S ELEPHANT
(Illustrated by Yoko Tanaka)

PAUL FEIG ("My Parents Gave My Bedroom to a Biker") is an acclaimed television writer, producer, and director. He created and wrote, along with friend Judd Apatow, the cult classic television show about high school life in the 80s, *Freaks and Geeks*. Since then, he has directed such shows as *The Office*, *Mad Men*, *30 Rock*, *Nurse Jackie*, and *Arrested Development*, in addition to two feature films, *I Am David* and *Unaccompanied Minors*. Paul has also written two memoirs and a children's book. He lives in Los Angeles.

SELECTED TITLE
IGNATIUS MACFARLAND: FREQUENAUT!

JACK GANTOS ("The Bloody Souvenir") is the celebrated author of JOEY PIGZA LOSES CONTROL, which received a Newbery Honor. He is also the author of the popular picture books about Rotten Ralph and JACK'S BLACK BOOK, the latest in his acclaimed series of semiautobiographical story collections featuring his alter ego, Jack Henry. His book HOLE IN MY LIFE was a Robert Seibert Honor Book and a Michael J. Printz Honor Book. Jack lives with his family in Boston, Massachusetts. You can read more about him online at www.jackgantos.com.

SELECTED TITLES
The Joey Pigza series, including
JOEY PIGZA SWALLOWED THE KEY

The Jack Henry series, including JACK ADRIFT:
Fourth Grade Without a Clue

The Rotten Ralph series, including THE NINE LIVES OF
ROTTEN RALPH

HOLE IN MY LIFE

THE LOVE CURSE OF THE RUMBAUGHS

JEFF KINNEY ("Unaccompanied Minors") is best known as the creator of the internet comic–turned–publishing sensation DIARY OF A WIMPY KID, which has spawned many sequels and a live-action movie. He lives in Massachusetts with his family. You can visit him online at www.wimpykid.com.

SELECTED TITLES
DIARY OF A WIMPY KID and its sequels: RODRICK RULES, THE LAST STRAW, and DOG DAYS

DAVID LUBAR ("Kid Appeal") is the author of many hilarious books for kids, including the Nathan Abercrombie: Accidental Zombie and Weenies series. He once had a goldfish that lived for seven years and grew to monstrous proportions. Besides writing, he worked for many years as a video game developer. He lives in Nazareth, Pennsylvania. You can find out more about him online at www.davidlubar.com.

SELECTED TITLES
Nathan Abercrombie, Accidental Zombie:
MY ROTTEN LIFE

IN THE LAND OF THE LAWN WEENIES:
And Other Warped and Creepy Tales

FLIP

HIDDEN TALENTS

PUNISHED!

ADAM REX ("Will") is the acclaimed *New York Times* best-selling author and illustrator of many books for kids. His middle grade novel THE TRUE MEANING OF SMEKDAY is currently under development as a feature film. He admits his favorite things are animals, spacemen, Mexican food, Ethiopian food, monsters, puppets, comic books, nineteenth-century art, skeletons, bugs, and robots, and lives in Arizona with his wife, who is a physicist. You can find out about these things and more online at www.adamrex.com.

SELECTED TITLES

FRANKENSTEIN MAKES A SANDWICH

FRANKENSTEIN TAKES THE CAKE

PSSST!

THE TRUE MEANING OF SMEKDAY

FAT VAMPIRE: *A Never Coming of Age Story*

DAVID YOO ("A Fistful of Feathers") is the acclaimed author of two YA novels, and his debut middle grade novel, THE DETENTION CLUB, is forthcoming. He spends his spare time staring or blinking (either in wonder or abject horror) at his newborn son, Griffin. He teaches in the MFA program at Pine Manor College and at the Gotham Writers' Workshop. David lives in Massachusetts. To see the creepiest-looking cat in the history of mankind, check out www.daveyoo.com.

SELECTED TITLES

STOP ME IF YOU'VE HEARD THIS ONE BEFORE

GIRLS FOR BREAKFAST